Tales from the Dragon's Lair

by
Reginald A Griffiths

✧✧✧✧

with illustrations by
Ann C Bryn-Evans

PublishAmerica
Baltimore

© 2004 by Reginald A Griffiths.
All rights reserved. No part of this book may be reproduced, stored in a retrieval system or transmitted in any form or by any means without the prior written permission of the publishers, except by a reviewer who may quote brief passages in a review to be printed in a newspaper, magazine or journal.

First printing

ISBN: 1-4137-7889-5
PUBLISHED BY PUBLISHAMERICA, LLLP
www.publishamerica.com
Baltimore

Printed in the United States of America

Contents

Love and Honour	-8-
The Woodsman's Tale	-18-
The Flower Lady	-34-
The Listening Chair	-50-
The Seeing Stone	-68-
Panda Ling	-82-
The Gift	-96-
The Bubble Man	-120-

Preface and Dedication

These stories were written for children who have not yet lost the knowledge we are all born with: the knowledge that all things are possible for those who understand that what we call the real world is actually not the real world. The world we live in is of make-believe, one that is actually the magic world of invention.

These stories are also for grown-up people who have forgotten the knowledge they were born with and, remembering, can once more resume the quest for that most important knowledge, the knowledge of oneself.

Ann Bryn-Evans is one of those who has not forgotten; she has used her skills to bring the stories to life with her beautiful illustrations.

This book is dedicated to my most important friend and teacher, Morgana, she who resides in the lair, the dragon, is the one who fires me with the inspiration to tell these tales.

Morgana is, in reality, a white witch—not the black kind whose spells make an evil world more evil, but a kind and benevolent witch who works quietly and mostly unseen, working to bring a little divine light into the darkness of ignorance.

I also wish to add my thanks to my dear friend Bill Jowett who has given his time and encouragement in word-processing and compiling this book so that children of all ages may enjoy the *Tales of the Dragon's Lair*.

Love and Honour

The little boy was fascinated by the forest that grew near the castle. Since the time his parents had died, his life had been one of ceaseless work, to the best of his ability, with the castle staff. They in turn watched out for him.

One day, as he was in the woodland glen, a very elegant old man came walking along the woodland path. The old man saw the little boy and, for a moment or two, watched him.

"Hi boy," shouted the old man, "come over here!"

The little boy looked up and went to him. He thought he knew the old man, but he wasn't sure.

"Yes sir," said the boy.

"What's your name, boy?" asked the old man gently.

"Dray," said the boy, "and who are you?" looking into the eyes of the old man.

"I'm the Lord of the Manor and this is my land as

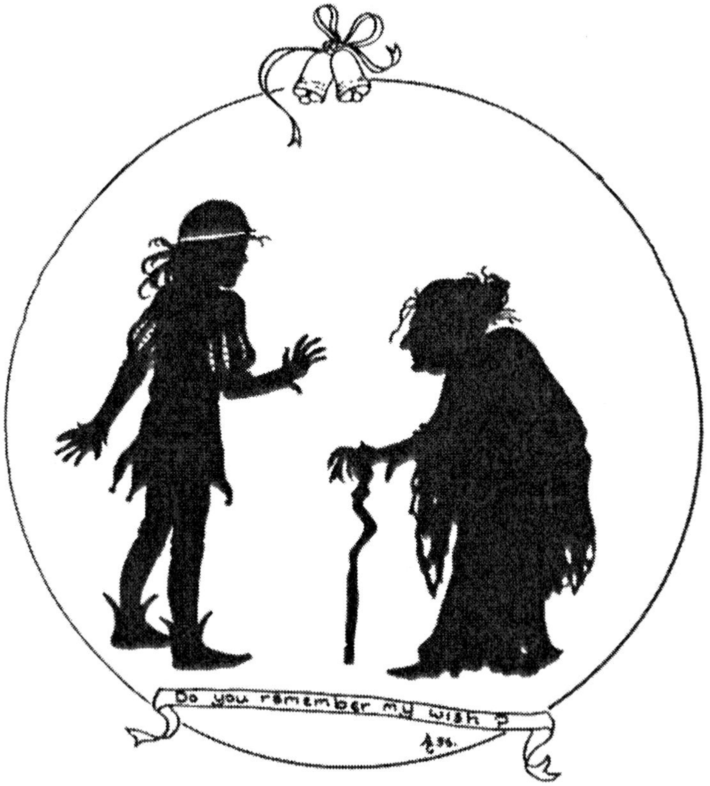
Do you remember my wish ?

far as the eye can see, Dray," he replied, waving his arm around in a circle. "I've seen you here before, and around the castle itself," said the old man. The boy explained that when he was little he had been orphaned and the servants at the castle had adopted him.

The old man smiled at him, for it wasn't a coincidence that he had met the boy, he had been watching him for a long time.

So the old man took to the boy Dray and over the next passing years taught him all about the ways of nature and how we all fit into the web of life, whether we be man, beast or plant.

"Each life form has its own beauty," said the old man, "and you must strive to find it for yourself. Give out love and love will come back. Always honour your word, no matter what. Through the two words of love and honour, you will see the beauty of life. Remember this well!"

The years passed and Dray, walking through his favourite part of the forest, was thinking of his forthcoming eighteenth birthday.

Suddenly, up ahead, he heard an awful deathly scream from somebody or something in deadly fear! As he turned a corner in the path, between two large trees he saw an old woman trying to fight off a large wild animal. He rushed forward and chased it away.

He turned and looked at the old woman: she was cowering from him. He looked at her and saw she was very ugly. Her face was covered with warts, she had no teeth and her white hair was dirty and matted. She was wearing a tattered old white robe that was torn in many places.

"Get away from me," she said, "I don't want anything from you, you're the same as other men."

Dray could feel the hatred coming from her. It was as if she had never had a kind deed done for her, or even a kind word spoken to her in all of her life.

"Don't touch me," spat the old woman. Dray ignored her and bent down to help her up. Though she must have been the most ugly woman he had ever seen, he recalled the words that the Lord of the Manor had taught him those many years ago: "You must find beauty in whatever lifeform you meet: it's there, for those with the eyes to see! Honour and love are the keys."

The old woman was looking at the young man as he helped her to her feet. *What a handsome man he is*, she thought. "You, young man, are the first who has ever showed me kindness!" she said aloud.

Although she smelt terrible, he managed to smile at her.

"Let me do you a service, young sir, what would you like?" she said.

Dray just laughed, as he had heard of wishes being granted, but he did not believe in them at all.

"Well, I see by your face you don't believe in wishes being granted," said the old woman.

"No, I don't," said Dray, "but I will tell you this— I'm so convinced it doesn't work that I will grant you a wish also!"

Dray then told the old woman what his wish was. "My wish is for two gifts only, one of wealth and the other of health. This way I can help other people less fortunate than myself and have no concern for my own welfare."

The old woman accepted the wish. "But," she continued, "for one of your wishes to be granted, somebody near to you must pay." Dray hesitantly agreed.

"Now," said the old woman, "here is my wish. I wish to have first offer of your hand in marriage!"

"What!" exclaimed Dray, staggered at the thought. "That's easy for you to say, but I've vowed never to get married, I've seen so many people made sad because of it!"

"But you promised, so you agree?" asked the old woman.

"Yes," said Dray, reconciled to his fate.

"Now I must go, as the sun is now setting. Remember your promise!" he heard her calling out as he made his way back to castle.

Eight years later, Dray was very busy going over the castle's accounts, checking to see that all was in order. As he sat back in his chair, his mind drifted back to the day when his adopted father had sent for him. He had been twenty-one at the time.

"My son, I'm dying. I have made a will and instructed the priest to ensure it is carried out. You, Dray," he continued, "must settle down. There are many a maiden you could take as your bride."

"But sir," replied Dray, "I'm happy just working and looking after you." *Anyway, you have many more years to go yet. You have out-lived the companion of your choice, even though she appeared very old when you were married,* thought Dray to himself.

The old man just smiled and then said, "Remember the two words, honour and love—remember them, Dray!"

Dray left the old man to rest. Two days later he died. Sadness fell over the land. He was loved and honoured by many of all stations in life. After the funeral, the old priest called together many high-ranking people of the land to read of the old man's wishes, as recorded in his will.

The priest wasted no time and read out all the little bequests first. There weren't any for Dray. Finally the priest turned to Dray and read the last part of the will. "To my son Dray I give all my wealth and may by doing so bring you health, these are my wishes to you."

Dray was taken aback, especially by the words—they sounded so familiar and yet he could not place them. All the gathered assembly cheered and clapped. They all agreed the old man could not have made a better choice for his successor as Lord of the Manor.

That seemed years ago and yet only five years had passed. Now Dray was Lord of the Manor, with lands as far as the eye could see.

One of the maidens, whose name was Astra, had greed in her heart and was determined to enchant Dray into marriage, if only to obtain control of his wealth. Over the next two years she schemed and weaved her love spells until one day, late in autumn as the leaves turned brown, she lured Dray into asking him to marry her.

The wedding day was set and people near and

afar were invited. Dray thought, *Well, the maiden could be a good wife for me and help run the castle estates.*

On the wedding day all the guests were assembled in the big church within the grounds of the castle.

Dray waited, and soon the trumpets sounded the arrival of Astra, his bride-to-be. She walked down the aisle and stood beside him. Dray turned to look at her and noticed she didn't have a smile on her face.

The priest welcomed all and, as he started the service, asked that they witness this day of joy. Five minutes into the ceremony the priest requested, "If anybody knows why these two people should not be joined together as man and wife, let him now speak or never speak again and dwell in peace."

Suddenly the church door flew open and everybody turned to look round. There stood an ugly old woman, dressed in a torn white robe. The old woman yelled, "He cannot marry that maiden, he promised to marry me!"

A hush fell over everybody present. Dray turned and looked on in horror. Who was this old ugly woman, what was she doing!

The priest beckoned the old woman forward and said to Dray, "My Lord, I think that we should take all parties to my private chambers so that we can resolve what this is all about."

Dray agreed, so his bride-to-be, her parents, high officials and the old woman followed the priest to his chambers and into a large room. Once inside the priest asked the old woman to explain why she had interrupted the service on this important day.

The old woman turned to Dray and said, "Do you remember when, in the forest, you were granted two wishes for wealth and health?"

Dray started to recall the day when, as a lad, he had met an old woman. Surely she couldn't be the same woman. He looked closely at her and yes, it was her, still just as ugly as the first day he had met her.

"Do you remember my wish?" continued the old woman. "You promised me first refusal in marriage to you. I now claim my wish!"

Dray was taken aback. Yes, he had promised. He turned to the priest and said. "She is right, I did promise her, I gave my word!"

The priest looked at Dray and could see that this was the time to be diplomatic. "My Lord," he said to Dray, "I have never known you to break a promise, and so the only solution is that you must marry this old woman." Dray agreed that was the only thing he could do. Astra, his bride-to-be, was furious and stormed out of the church.

An announcement was made and the congregation gathered sat in silence as the priest married the old woman to Dray. After the ceremony the couple left the church. The old woman chuckled and said to Dray, "I can't wait for when the sun sets and it's our first night."

Dray was very depressed, but he had always honoured his word, as he had been told to do by the Lord of the Manor when he was a young lad. It was true—he had got his wish of wealth and health.

The sun set and the time came for Dray and his bride to retire to their honeymoon room. The door closed behind him and they were alone. The old woman dragged herself towards the bed, and she laid upon it. "Well, my husband," said the old lady, "are you pleased that I'm your bride?"

Dray turned towards her and said, "Old woman, I knew not your name was Diana until this day, but although I've kept my promise, I cannot love you. You do not have youth or beauty, so how can I love you in such form as you are in?"

The old woman sat up and looked directly at Dray. "Well, Dray," she said, "you once gave me kindness many years ago, so I will do the same to you, but for your eyes only. How would you like me to be, would you like me to be like this?"

Suddenly the old woman changed into the most beautiful lady he had ever seen. "If you wish I will stay as this, or as a maiden, or a mother, or as whatever your heart desires."

Dray was spellbound. He said, "May I call you Diana?"

"Yes," she replied, "after all, we are married." The words seemed to laugh upon her lips. She was so beautiful.

"I would like you to help me love you so that I can honour and love you truly, for many years ago I was told that I would see beauty in all if I honour and love truthfully."

Diana laughed and pulled him towards her. Her whole body radiated love for husband Dray, Lord of the Manor. She loved him and he loved her.

She said, "I will be your companion for many years."

The Lord of the Manor was very happy and all his people accepted his companion.

One day a message was rushed to him to return post haste. When he arrived he was told that his companion, Diana, had suddenly died and before she collapsed she had been writing a letter to him. He read the letter quietly. She had written: "I will always be with you, for love conquers all, my beloved."

It seemed like only yesterday, but already five years had passed. To get rid of his sadness he decided to walk in the forest. As he walked along the woodland trail he saw a little boy. He stopped and watched him for a few moments. "Hi boy," he shouted "come here." The little boy looked up and came to him. He thought he knew the old man, but he wasn't sure.

"Yes sir," said the boy. The Lord of the Manor looked at the boy who he had seen working in or about the stables, and said, "I think that you and I need to talk." With that the Lord of the Manor took the boy's hand tenderly and started to walk the path back to the castle.

A Woodsman's Tale

The old man Briggs walked down the gangplank for the last time, not as sprightly as he had been fifty years ago. It seemed as if all his life had been spent walking gangplanks. He was always either going or coming from a place and as he looked up at the gangplank once more, it was as if a bridge of memories were held there.

His greatest memory of the past years was of the last time he saw his wife, Mary, who had died without giving birth. Her face was still glowing and yet he felt that although he would never look up or down a gangplank again, she was smiling with that coming-home smile only she could show.

It was her wish that he should give up the sea life, but in the end she knew that it was in his blood. As he said once, to her, "The sea is magic, and that's what gives me energy."

He turned away and headed towards the town centre.

the two birds that he had just finished carving

The Company of Pan & Sons had been acting as practising solicitors for many years and some say that they had formulated the town's original charter hundreds of years ago. They claimed that their offices dealt with many estates buying and selling properties. The firm had been passed from father to son, through time itself.

Today, Mr Pan, senior was expecting an old man, a Mr William Briggs, to complete the purchase on a property fifteen miles out of town. *A nice retirement cottage, it should suit him,* thought Mr. Pan, he also having been at sea all of his life.

Mr Pan knew it was a charming place with its own two acres, including a picturesque wood. It was funny since as far back as he could remember, this firm, even when his late father before him was in charge, had always handled this cottage.

Since the late Mr James White had died some fifty years ago, it seemed that the place just wouldn't sell, and was waiting for somebody special.

Well, today it was looking as though that somebody had arrived. For here, out of his office window, in the street below he could see old man Briggs taking an envelope from his pocket and reading the letter inside.

Old Briggs rechecked the address: "Messrs Pan & Son, Solicitors of Law, 27 Willow Lane, Barking on Sea, Cornwall."

"Right," he said to himself, "let's get under way."

The outside of the building seemed as if it had been there since the beginning of time. It was old and weather-beaten and yet had a touch of beauty of its own. He opened the old wooden door and went in.

He felt as he entered that time had stood still. There was a large stairway leading gracefully up to the next floor above. Although the building looked old, it smelt as if it was clean and polished every day. He went up the stairs and there was a large brass plate inscribed "Messrs Pan & Son, Solicitors of Law." He tapped upon the old oak door and then, as if they were waiting for him, the door opened to reveal a tall elderly man.

"My name is Mr William Briggs and I have an appointment with a Mr Pan," stated the old man.

"I am Mr Pan," replied the man, "do come in, Mr Briggs. Would you care for a drink, or anything?"

"Yes please, but will you drop the 'Mr' business? Everybody calls me Willy."

Mr Pan smiled and replied, "My name is John."

Mr Pan explained the cottage over a cup of tea, and how it had been empty for some time. He told Mr. Briggs how it had become a bit overgrown since the beginning of March, probably due to all the rain they had been having over the last few weeks.

Mr Pan told Mr Briggs he could just move in now and possibly "live in" it whilst he got the place fitted up.

Willy thanked him. "Don't worry," he told Mr Pan, "I've slept in worse places before, and now that I've retired, I've got all the time in the world to get my land legs back. I've also made all the arrangements for a builder and supplies over the week or so. I hope there's a phone there."

"Of course," said John, "I have already arranged to have it connected. If you like, I will run you over there today and help you to settle in."

Willy gratefully accepted the offer, and they set off together in John's car.

As they neared the place, John told Willy a little about the place and how the local people believed it to be haunted. "They say they have seen a man pottering about in the garden, but I've checked it out and there's nobody there. You can see the place as you come around the bend, half a mile ahead," John said.

Willy listened to the history of the place and was lost in time until John said, "Look, there it is!"

Willy looked and saw the old place—it was just like an old boat that's been docked and forgotten. He fell in love with it and could have sworn that he felt a "Hi" come from it.

They got out of the car and he felt just like he had come home, when of course in reality, he had never been in the area in all of his life. He had simply answered an advert he had seen in the paper, and bingo, everything had gone well, just as if he was meant for it.

He unloaded his belongings from John's car along with all the temporary provisions he had procured to tide him over the next few days. He thanked John, as the solicitor had to get back, but he promised that he would drop in to see Mr Briggs in a day or so.

"Thanks John," said Willy, waving goodbye, "I'll be all right."

Willy put the kettle on for a mug of tea, a habit that he had always had—not that he didn't like cups, but as they say, old habits die hard. As he supped his mug of tea, he looked around his new home.

"What would Mary think of this place?" he mused to himself. He took his mug of tea into the garden to look around. As he went out of the back door, he could see to his left an old lawn that had been left to run wild.

In the garden were some large stones that in the past could have been used as sitting stones. *I'll have to bring them to life*, he thought. To his right was more of a tidy lawn but it had old bushes here and there. At the bottom was an old wooden gate that led down to the wooded area of his garden.

Phew! he thought. *I've got a lot of work to get this place ship-shape.*

He was turning to go back into the house when he noticed a movement near the bottom fence. He stopped to look again, but there was nobody there. "I could have sworn there was somebody or something there!"

Back inside the house, he made notes of what had to be done and in what order. In a back room, he pulled an old table to one side and there he found an old box.

He discovered that the box wasn't locked, and upon opening it, he found a full set of woodcarving tools. "Somebody took a pride in their tools—fancy the last owner not taking them when he left the house."

He could appreciate the quality of the tools, being a man of the sea, for he himself had always liked to carve wood to whittle away the time at sea. *I'll get them out later, and maybe use them*, he thought.

Willy settled down nicely and after six weeks he had the house and garden looking something of the way he wished them to be. He lit his old pipe and went to sit in the garden.

It was such a lovely day. He was gently taking in the wonders of Mother Earth when he saw a man at the edge of the wood.

"Hi, Willy!" shouted the man. "Nice day, isn't it?" The man stopped and looked across at Willy. He then approached the garden fence. "You're the new owner, aren't you?" he asked.

"Aye," said Willy. "Do you live hereabouts?" Willy was not at all angry that the man was in or about his wood. He felt attuned to the stranger as if they were sailors meeting on the vast ocean of life, both with the same common beliefs.

"Yes," replied the man, "just beyond the wood. My name is Michael."

Willy asked Michael if he would like a cup of tea. Michael replied that he would prefer a mug. Well, that was it—instant friendship seemed to have been struck up.

"What do you do, Michael?" asked Willy. "You seem a young looking person, but you have an oldish outlook on life."

"Well," Michael replied, "I'm a herbalist, which means I study and make up potions and remedies to help people and animals. More of a hobby, you might say. What do you like doing, Willy?" he asked.

"Well, I'm a bit of a whittler—no, not a moaner, I like to carve wood to make something. You see, being at sea all my life, I couldn't have anything big and permanent with me, so I whittled wood. After my wife died, I felt a bit adrift, as you might say, but I finally decided to get back to land, to find earth as they say. That is why I retired from the sea," Willy replied.

"Well then, I will have to get some wood for you to carve into, say, an animal, and you can put it in your garden. Maybe you could finish up with a garden of wooden statues," Michael said, laughing.

Willy thought about this. What an idea, a garden of carved people—his own family, as he had none of his own.

"Yes, that would be fine, Michael, what a good idea. I could sit outside and carve and carve to my heart's content. Tell me, Michael, about your herbs. Did you have to go to a college of something to learn about them?"

"No, Willy, the knowledge has been passed down to me from generations. Why are you interested?"

"Well, except for the odd herb my Mary used to pop into her cooking, I don't know anything about them."

"Right, next time I call, I'll bring some books and tell you about my magical world of herbs, but now I must be off."

With that he hopped over the fence and was away.

Over the next couple of weeks, Willy got out the

old tool box to see what was there. He had got himself a nice piece of wood and started carving away.

The tools seemed as if they had a will of their own, and soon he was carving small objects of his desire. It seemed that he had only to think of the finished object he desired and in no time the tools were carving away under the guidance of his hands.

Willy was thinking of Michael and his herbs, wondering whether he would be seeing him again, when there was a knock at the door. He opened it, and there stood Michael laughing his head off.

"Well," he said, "I've brought a few logs in for you to carve, Willy."

Willy looked over his friends shoulder, and there he saw a pile of large logs, some as long as six feet and about two feet wide. How on earth had Michael managed to get them into the garden without him hearing?

"Come in, Michael," said Willy. "I was just thinking about you. Look—I want to show you something. What do you think about these?" Willy picked up the two birds he had just finished carving yesterday.

"My, those are so lifelike, I feel as though they're real. But may I make a suggestion? Why don't you put a copper rod into the middle of each of them, and then you could put them into the garden earth? Also, if you put two crystals in as eyes, they would appear even more real than they do now."

Willy considered this, and thought, *Why stop at this?* He could have his own family of people. He had heard on his travels abroad that crystals had healing properties.

Yes, that was it—he would call them his healing family. If he had any visitors to his house who were sick, they could touch and feel his carvings, which would have crystals in different parts of their bodies for different ailments. The copper could be an energy source for them.

Willy thought for a moment—how he did get such ideas! Such ideas developed into projects that only he could bring to maturity.

Then the next thought hit him. Why not ask Michael to place herbs around each carving, so that people could benefit from him? The herbs could help all people or animals—in fact, come to think of it, they could help all life forms.

Willy told Michael of his thoughts, and he agreed to join in on the project on the condition that his name would not be used and neither would money be asked for. All he asked was that Willy provide a box for people to drop coins into. Things were finalised, and over the following six months, all went well.

John the estate agent dropped in to see how Willy was getting on. He was amazed by how things had gone since he had last seen Willy. He was so impressed with Willy's work that he asked if he would pass the word around to people.

"Fine," said Willy, "but remember, no money. Nothing is for sale, I will only give these as gifts."

Over the next two years Willy's name became well known; his family was photographed and his activities reported in many newspapers. He also noticed how he was becoming familiar with Michael's herbs and their properties.

One day Willy felt awful and just could not get out of bed, no matter how he tried. He was sweaty and felt no life in him. Was the earth pulling him down, draining him? He heard Michael come into the house.

"Willy, where are you?"

"Up here in bed. I feel so ill."

Michael saw the state of his friend, laid out in his bed. He was concerned. "Don't worry, Willy. I will fetch some of my herbs, and you will be fine very shortly."

He rushed away and later arrived back with some herbs Willy had never seen before. "Chew these," he said. "They will help you."

The leaves Michael gave him tasted sweetish. "What are they?" Willy asked.

"Trade secret, Willy," he said, smiling. "You'll be all right by the afternoon."

Michael stayed with his friend until the herbs had done their work.

Willy laid back, thinking about all that had happened since he had come to the house.

Suddenly, he swore he could hear voices outside the house. "Michael, do we have visitors?" he asked.

"No, not really, Willy. Don't worry, just rest."

Willy closed his eyes and slept.

When he awoke it was late evening and the sun was about to set.

All was quiet and he realised that in all the time

he had known Michael, this was the first time Michael had been with him when dusk began to fall. Michael brought Willy some drink and food on a tray and could he could see that Willy looked a lot better.

"Thank you, Michael," said Willy, "for looking after me. It's funny—my Mary would have done the same thing as you did, fussing around me."

Michael put the tray down and told Willy he would see him tomorrow.

"Why not stay the night?" Willy asked.

"Sorry," Michael replied, "I've got a lot of things that must be done, see you."

At this point he disappeared out of the back door and was away.

It seemed even stranger to Willy that he did not even know where Michael lived. Whenever he asked, Michael would just say "over there," pointing to the edge of the wood.

The following day the sun shone down onto the garden and Willy felt fine as he sat on the sitting stones drinking his tea. The herbs had certainly done the trick to get him well.

Michael came back a few days later and said he was sorry for not having come over sooner. "How are you feeling now?" he asked.

"Couldn't be better—I feel like a young lad on a boat that's just had a major overhaul."

Willy threw himself into his carving even more: it seemed as if his carvings of people were alive. He gave them each a name and felt sure that as he talked to them, carving life into them, they came alive.

He brushed these thoughts from his mind, maybe they were just the ravings of an old man.

One day he had a visitor from the local children's home. Hid visitor asked if a small party of children could come to visit his garden and see the wooden statues.

In the past Willy had not had time for children since he and Mary could not have any, and what with living on his own, had not given them any thought.

Today seemed different. The head teacher of the home really appeared to be a loving person who cared for the children, so he agreed to allow a limited number of them to visit next week.

The following Tuesday a small band of six children arrived and were shown around. They were all fascinated by the statues and animal carvings.

One of the boys, whose name was Tommy Farr, could not take his eye off the statue Willy had carved in the likeness of Michael. The boy kept looking at the statue and then to the end of the garden.

"That's the man at the end of the garden, the man who said for you to make this statue?" he said.

"Yes," replied Willy.

It suddenly dawned upon Willy that this boy could see Michael. Nobody had ever seen Michael except him.

When the day ended the boy just did not want to leave the garden. "Come along, Tommy, we must go now," said the teacher. The boy looked up into Willy's eyes and said he would be back one day. Willy believed he would.

Willy decided he had to ask Michael why he was so much of a mystery to everybody. When his friend arrived, he asked, "Michael, why is it that nobody sees you?"

"Well, it's like this," the herbalist replied. "Only the pure in heart and those of earth can see me. Like you yourself, who has discovered the wonders of earth, that boy Tommy is one such person."

Willy simply sat back and thought about what Michael had said. Why him? He had to agree that since meeting Michael his life had been so enriched, he was so lucky. He hoped their friendship would continue for many years to come.

The visit from the boy seemed to have happened years ago, but now he was feeling his age. Michael never seemed to age, was he the magic of the house?

As he encountered this profound thought, he felt a pain in his chest. It hurt. He lost feeling and then the room seemed to go round about his head, then darkness. It was but a flash of time, but as he opened his eyes, there was Michael looking over him.

"Come Willy, my friend, let's get you onto that chair." Michael looked at him and, speaking gently, said, "Willy, the time has come for you to meet somebody."

Michael helped Willy up and walked him out of the back door and into the garden.

Suddenly Michael let go of him; Willy felt so well and secure. He then noticed that his family of wooden creations was no longer in the garden. Then he noticed to his left a woman sitting on one of his stones. Her face looked familiar, although he could not place it.

Then the woman spoke. Well Willy, you have now found your earth magic—it isn't like your sea magic."

Willy could not believe it, for as she turned around he realised it was Mary, his Mary, as she had been when they first met.

"Mary, Mary," he cried, "is it really you?"

"Yes Willy, it's really me, and we will be together for evermore."

At that he heard laughter behind him. He saw Michael leading all his family to join him. They were alive! He now had all he had ever wished for. He looked back towards the house and then he saw that the sign above it wasn't reading "Latrop" anymore, but "Portal."

"Yes," said Michael, "you have now passed through your own portal of life into the happiness of eternal life."

At the office of Pan & Sons, old John Pan had passed on many years ago and now his son Peter and Peter's son Paul were running the business.

"Paul," said his father, "I'm expecting a prospective buyer for that old house that used to belong to old Mr Briggs. Funny the way he died, wasn't it? They found him just sitting in the garden like a statue, as if he was asleep. He had a smile on his face. I would love to die the way he did, happy. Anyway, when he comes, show him directly to my office, will you?"

"Yes," said Peter, "but Father, what is the new man's name?"

"Oh yes, sorry," said his father, "his name is Thomas Farr."

The Flower Lady

Nancy Watson felt down in the dumps. *I don't know why, but ever since my Tommy died I just haven't got the get up and go in me any more*, she thought to herself. Pulling herself out of her favourite chair, she made herself a cup of tea. "Come on, Nancy old girl, get your togs on and let's get out: maybe a walk round that old market will cheer you up," she said to herself.

The old market had been going for many a year and it was known far and wide as the Peoples' Market, where you could buy nearly anything you wanted at a price ordinary people could afford. Traders came and went over the years, but others were family businesses, passed on from one generation to the next.

This day there were a few new stall holders arriving to sell their wares. Old Mrs Watson walked round on her favourite route. Many market folk had

A talking plant, whatever next?

gotten to know her well and she always had a cheerful word for each. They remembered when she used to come round with her old man Tommy, who was just as cheerful as she was. They said that she was like an unofficial granny for those who worked at the market. As she wandered around an old man at a new stand beckoned her over to him.

"Hello," he said, "you look down in the dumps."

Cheeky, she thought, *but it's true—I am feeling a bit sorry for myself and it must show.* "Hello," she replied, "I've not seen you here before."

"No," the vendor replied, "that's right, I tend to travel around visiting markets and doing a little bit of selling here and there."

She had noticed that he did not have much to sell, his was like a white elephant stand if anything. Still, today she was not here to buy anything but simply to browse.

"By the way, what's your name, the name you are known by?" she asked.

"Hopkins, or Jack to my friends," he replied. "In fact, I believe my family goes back to a very well known gentleman of the middle 17th century, he was a sort of a general," he added. "Anyway lady, you can call me Jack, what do you go by?"

"Nancy," she replied.

"Well Nancy, my old dad used to say to me that if a person is down in the dumps, the only way for them to get out of it is for them to have a goal for something and to go for it, and by looking at you, it looks like you need something to go for, for yourself."

How right he is, thought Nancy. *It seems as if he is reading my thoughts deep down inside of me, him being a stranger, yet not a stranger.*

"Look Nancy, I got an idea. You need something to look forward to." He took out an old box from under the stall and from within it he pulled out a faded packet of seeds. "It's not much, but if you plant these it will give you a goal to go for. Only thing is, I've had them for some time and the packet has faded, so I don't know what they are."

"What a good idea, Jack! I will call them our hope seeds, as they will give me something to hope for—to look forward to, as you might say."

When Nancy got home she went to her little garden. It wasn't big, just a little piece of ground she Tommy had made for her to grow her "bits and bobs" in, as he used to say.

She opened the pack and found only one seed in it. *Well,* she thought, *I've never known a packet of seeds to contain only one seed!*

She set about and planted the seed with great care, almost as if she was caring for a child: her child, perhaps, the one she and Tommy had never had.

❖❖❖❖

Each day she watered the seed and about a week later, a little green shoot appeared. She knelt down and whispered, "Welcome to this world, my little one, I'm your plant mother. My goodness—if anybody could see me talking to this plant they would think that I'm mad!"

The days passed, the shoot grew and grew, and one day a flower appeared. She looked at the flower with its five blue petals that seem to radiate life and she thought, *How beautiful you are, I'm so pleased that I'm the one who helped you to grow!*

The next instant she heard a voice say to her, "Thank you, my plant mother." She looked around and could not see anybody, yet she could have sworn that somebody had spoken. "I'm here, in the ground, you put me here, I'm yours."

She looked down at the plant and said, "Was that you speaking to me?"

"Yes," the plant said, "why are you so surprised when you yourself have been talking to me all of my lifetime?"

Well I never! she thought. *A talking plant, whatever next? How does it manage to talk to me? It seems as though its voice is in my head.* "Who—or what—are you? Do you have a name?" she asked.

"Yes," the plant replied, "it's Barcool, and I'm not what you would call a female or a male in your world. In mine, I'm a promulgator. I can, if conditions are right, travel from my world to yours to help you. My world is much more advanced than yours in some things, yet in others we are still learning.

"Our worlds are not above or below each other, but are parallel—sort of side by side, if you see what I mean." The voice in her head went on. "We have been aware of your world long before man was born.

"At times we become aware of certain people who have a need we can fill for them, and you are one of those people. You see, when a person in your world becomes sad, their sadness sometimes reflects into our world and thus unbalances the life forces of the universe."

"This is all very well, all these worlds you talk about, but what has it to do with me?" she asked.

"Nancy—you don't mine me calling you by your first name?"

"No," she said, for she was very happy to be talking to this plant, as it gave her a sense of being needed, something that had not happen since Tommy died. "You carry on, Barcool, it seems as if I have known you all my life."

"As you are probably aware, many people of your world talk to their plant life, especially the flowers, and it has been shown that the plants react to the sound of the voice of a human. We of our world want to help your world to join with our world to save both of our worlds."

Nancy sat still and tried to take in all Barcool had said. *Why me, I'm nobody,* she thought, *just an old lady alone.*

Barcool, who had been reading her thoughts, answered her, "You are somebody, you are a carer. Over the years we in my world have felt your concern for people and after the death of your Tommy, we had hoped that after a time you would get over what you call bereavement and you would start to get back to being your normal self.

"Alas, it hadn't happened as we had hoped, so

we—or I should say I—have arranged my 'birth' into your world to help you to start living again."

Nancy was amazed by what she was hearing. *Me, a carer! Well, I've always cared for people*, she thought. *He is right, I have not got back to my old self since Tommy died, maybe Barcool can help me.* "Right," said Nancy, "then what is your idea? I'm not going to spend the rest of my days sitting in this garden talking to a flower!"

Barcool laughed—well, his stem shook a bit.

He started to tell Nancy of his plan.

"Firstly, you are right, you have got to pot me so I can be with you in your home. There you can look after me. I will be regenerating and changing the earth you put into my pot so that it has a special property to heal. As you take the earth out you can put more back in and I will make this special compound for you. I know that you see people around you who need a helping hand, some whom your doctors cannot help anymore.

"This is where we help. My lifespan with you will be short compared with your lifespan, but I know that you are the one who can take some of the sadness out of your world, the sadness that affects mine."

Nancy smiled to herself at the thought of a Florence Nightingale with a bit of earth in her hand, but he was right, she did care for people and she could immediately think of two people who were really ill.

"Yes, I will do it," she said as Jack had said at the market, "we must have something to go for."

Barcool smiled to himself and she did likewise, for now they had got used to the fact that they were linked together, as if with common thoughts: she no longer needed to speak normally.

"Right, Barcool, let's get you potted." With no more to do, she dug him up, potted him, and took him indoors. "I will site you near the window so that you get plenty of sunlight," she said to him.

Over the next week she watered and cared for Barcool, making sure that all was to his liking.

"Barcool," she said, "tomorrow I'm going to see an old friend of mine who has a sick little boy; he has a rare illness that has made his hand crippled. The boy is now nine I believe. Tell me—would the earth help him? The doctors have given up on him."

Barcool shook his petals in a laughing manner and said, "Take a little bit from the pot and let me know how you get on."

✣✣✣✣

"Hello Jane, how is your little Peter getting on now?" she asked after arriving at her friend's house, for she had not seen them for over six months.

"All right really," she replied, "but it does make me sad to think of him with his poor hand the way it is. His friends don't seem to want to play with him because of it. I wish the doctors could help him."

"Jane," Nancy said, "let me tell you a story and maybe your Peter might get better."

Nancy told her all that had happened over the last few months and then sat back to study her friend's face. "Well, what do you think about that then?" asked Nancy.

Nancy's friend thought she was joking, but she knew Nancy would never tell lies. "Well indeed you may ask, what a to-do, do you think it could really help him?"

Jane went and fetched Peter. Between them they put some of the earth onto his hands. Young Peter thought it was a great game, playing with mud. After they wrapped his hands up they told him it would only be for a day or so, and then maybe he would be able to play with the other boys.

A thought passed through Nancy's mind: *Barcool never told me how long it would take to see the effect: I hope I have not made a fool of myself!*

As she thought of this a voice came into her head, saying: *Have a cup of tea, then take the wrappings off—trust me.* The voice sounded like Barcool's, but Nancy wondered how he could be speaking to her when he was at home? *Trust me*, the voice said again.

After about half an hour, Jane called her son to her. "Peter, could I check that those wrappings are all right?" She looked at the wrappings and saw that they seemed loose. "Silly old mum, I will have to take them off and put them on again," she said to him.

As she took the wrappings off, she caught her breath: There were his fingers, all straight and looking normal! "Nancy—look, look," she cried, "I have never seen his hands like this in all of his life, it's a miracle, that's what it is: a miracle!"

The tears poured from as she sobbed in happiness. "Oh thank you, Nancy, for making this the best day of my life."

Peter danced around waving his 'new' hand for all to see. "Look Mummy, it's just like anybody else's!" he said, and with that he ran outside to show everybody his new hand.

Nancy was warm and happy inside and said her goodbyes, saying that she must go now. With a wave she left Jane and rushed off home to tell Barcool all about it.

"Barcool, Barcool," Nancy shouted as she rushed into her front room, "it worked, his hand is better!"

"Steady Nancy, you don't need to shout, I was there with you in your mind, so to speak," said Barcool.

She stopped and looked at the flower and realised he had been there. How, she could not work out, but she knew what he said was true.

"But could it be, with you here and me there?"

"Well, you remember that I said we were one? This I can do because your thoughts are linked to mine, so that wherever you are, I am with you. What you did today makes me and my world feel good, so I am going to take you into my world, so that we can grow closer to each other in the work we feel you want to do.

"If at any time you feel funny, as you say, tell me. Now, Nancy, sit back in your chair and close your eyes. Feel peace come over you and I will try and show you my world in your language and understanding."

Nancy relaxed and then saw (or was it felt?) a warm sunny day, and than there was a very tall handsome man next to her. "Don't be frightened, Nancy, it's me, Barcool—I'm in this form so you can feel at ease.

"Now, Nancy, hold my hand and jump with me."

Suddenly the sunlight changed to all the colours of the rainbow and it was beautiful, it felt like swimming inside a bubble. Slowly they seemed to stop and all around was the sound of bells, little bells gently ringing all different sounds that seem to blend to the colours.

"Barcool," she said, "this place—where is it? It is like a dream where time stands still."

Barcool turned to her and said, "This is my world, where all is possible. It is unending, where harmony is the order of the day. It takes a lot of work to keep it like this but we try to do our best. You see, when a sad soul of your world is depressed it filters into our world. Thank goodness your world sends flowers to people who are not well, just to cheer them up."

Nancy could understand now how he felt, for this place was wonderful. Just then she noticed a pulsating blue bubble that seemed to glow. It gave out no heat, but more of a loving feeling.

"What's that blue bubble over there?" she asked.

"Ah yes—well, to put it into your words, it's a maternity hospital." He laughed. "What it does is care for the young seedlings' souls, so that when a seed is planted the little roots go down into the earth and there are united with its soul—its spirit, you might say—so as the plant grows its life form grows as well.

"I was in there once and I left when a pair of loving hands planted my body. The rest you know." He smiled at her. "Now, Nancy, it's time for us to go back to your world, for we have a lot of work to do to keep this balance here."

She did not want to leave, but the next moment she was sitting up in her chair smiling at her plant and feeling tired. "Thank you, Barcool, for letting me see your world, but it has made me very tired so I am off to my bed."

As she drifted off to sleep she had a thought: *I wonder if Barcool ever sleeps.*

As she closed her eyes she heard a gentle reply, "*Yes, I do—goodnight, Nancy.*"

⋄⋄⋄⋄

Over the next months Nancy helped a lot of her friends, those she felt needed that something extra. One day there was a knock on her door, and she opened it to see an old man bent over doubled.

"Excuse me," he said, "but is your name Nancy?"

"Yes," she said, "what can I do for you?"

"Look at me!" he cried. "Help me to walk upright once more, I know you can do it, I've heard it said!"

Nancy felt sorry for him so she invited him into her front room. "Now tell me your name."

"It's Jimmy," he said.

"Well Jimmy, go and sit on that stool over there and roll up your shirt so that I can see your back."

She could see how much his back was arched and that he must be in great pain. She went to the pot and laid some earth on him and told him to sit still for a while.

After an hour Jimmy asked if he could get up as his legs had gone to sleep

"As you wish," replied Nancy, "but be careful as you get up."

Jimmy reached for his stick, as he always did. As he raised himself he felt all of his backbones click and, to his amazement, he stood upright for the first in many a year.

"Nancy, look, I can stand up, I'm standing!" He danced around and around Nancy, and he could not thank her enough.

"Go on, wear my carpet out with your jumping around—would you mind jumping about outside my house so I can get some work done?"

Jimmy was so happy when he left Nancy that he just danced around the park all day and kept singing the praises of Nancy.

She kept popping down to the market to see if old Jack was there, but nobody had seen him since she herself had last been there, the day he had given her the seed. She so much wanted to tell him all about Barcool and the great and wonderful things that had happened to her.

She had been meaning to ask Barcool to help her as she had not been feeling too well of late, "probably all this running around I'm doing, but it seems that other people are more important."

The word had now got around about what Nancy was doing and many more people were asking for her help. She had to turn some away or else she wouldn't have any peace.

The next day was going to be a special day, as it marked six months since Barcool had come to flower, or as she put it, "come to age." She was also planning on showing her flower to a dear friend of hers on this anniversary, so she was really looking forward to the next day.

She sat in her chair and rested herself before doing those last chores around the house, after which she was going to make herself a nice drink before going to bed.

She put her drink down and suddenly she felt so very tired indeed, that she closed her eyes and then she sensed somebody near her, yet nobody came into the room.

She opened her eyes and sat upright, not believing what she was seeing. "Is that you, Tommy, is that really you?"

"Yes Nancy, it is me. I thought you needed a break, so I've been waiting for you to doze off before coming back to see you. Come on, old girl, let's you and me be off."

The following morning, Nancy's friend Mrs White knocked on Nancy's door but there was no reply. Mrs White kept knocking. "Still no reply, strange," her friend said to herself, "she is normally out and about by this time of the day." She then tried the handle and found the door open, so she walked in.

"Nancy, are you there? It's Jean here."

There was still no reply, so she walked into the main room and stopped when she saw Nancy slumped in her chair. She could see that her friend was dead, but she had a peaceful smile on her face, so happy looking, just as if she was dreaming.

Mrs White looked around the room and there in front of the window was a pot. The plant in this pot lay withered and dead on top of the earth.

Nancy is no longer with us, the flower lady is gone.

※※※※

Mary Wilson felt down in the dumps. *I don't know why, but ever since my Harry died I just haven't got the get up and go in me any more,* she thought to herself.

Pulling herself out of the favourite chair, she made herself a cup of tea. "Come on, Mary old girl, get your togs on and let's get out: maybe a walk round that old market will cheer you up," she said to herself.

The Listening Chair

There was a knock at the door of the old man's flat. He got up from his old wooden chair to answer it.

"Excuse me, are you Mr John Cane?" asked the young man standing in front of his door.

"Yes I am, what can I do for you?"

"Well, I have been asked to deliver a chair to you by a firm of solicitors, along with this letter. It looks like somebody has left it to you in their will. Anyway, can I bring it up whilst you are reading the letter? My mate and myself have to get back to the warehouse before five: we are already a hour behind on our deliveries."

"Why, a chair, it looks a bit worn and old! Who would want to leave me a chair of all things? Yes, of course, please bring it up," he said to the young man.

He opened the envelope and began to read the

i could spend hours in this chair

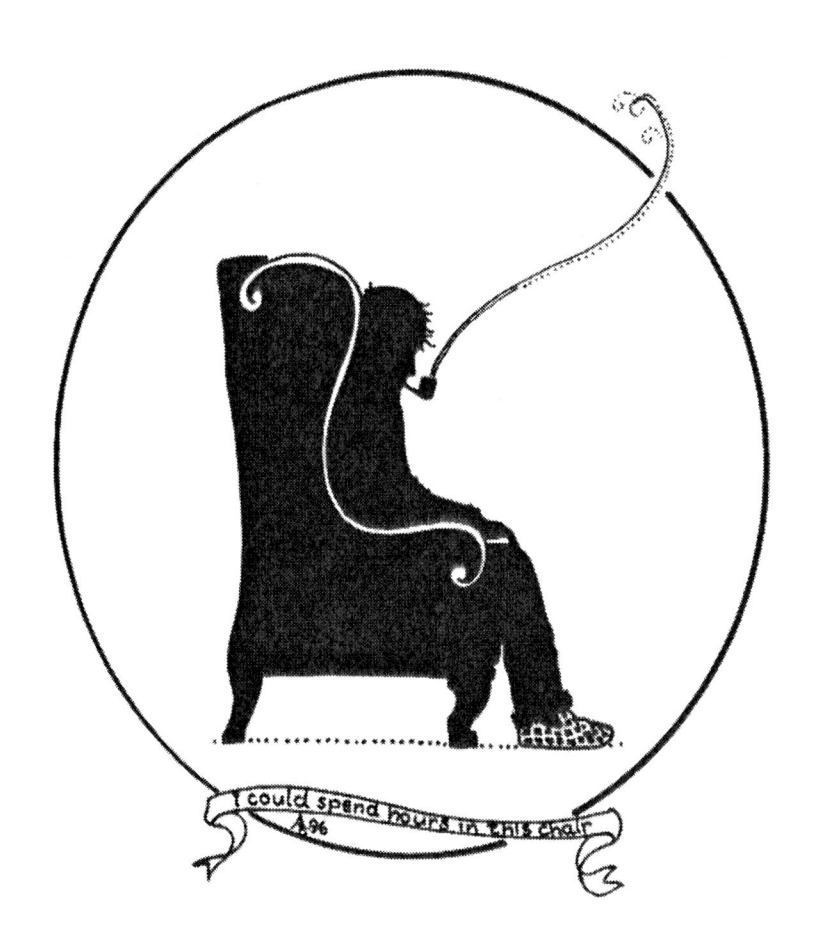

letter. "Dear Mr John Cane, you may not remember me, but about ten years ago we met on a park bench. I was that old smelly tramp—you offered part of your lunch to me, a perfect stranger."

John's memory started to race back and did recall a meeting with an old man by the name of Peter.

He continued to read the letter. "Well, you may recollect that my name was Peter and that at the time I was not in the best of spirits. You took time out to help me and from that help I picked myself up and went on to make something of my life—thanks to you.

"I managed to get a job and later, a place of my own in the country, just as you said I could do. You, and only you, had faith in me and on account of this I would like you to have something that came into my possession in a very strange way. One day you will know how!

"As you will have gathered, you are reading this after my death, and my solicitor has acted upon my instructions. I don't have much money but this chair, I assure you, will change your life. Please look after it and you will find that the chair will polish itself! Furthermore, if you keep it polished, it will become your chair in more ways than you can imagine."

The letter was signed: "Your old and grateful friend, Peter."

John did recall that day, for he had felt really sorry for the old boy. Peter had been a lot older than himself and yet he felt that Peter needed a fatherly talking to—something he believed had not happened before in Peter's life.

"Excuse me, Mr Cane, where would you like me to put it?" asked the delivery man, who was struggling with a large old leather armchair.

"Oh sorry," said John, "just put it through there, in my front room."

The delivery man carried it through and put it next to the window. It seemed to fit there, just what was wanted to finish off the old man's room. "Although it looks old, it still looks good just there, Mr Cane, just as if was made for the job. It is certainly a different sort of chair, and believe me, I've seen many chairs in my days."

Yes, the young man was right, it did seem to fit nicely just where he had put it, next to the window.

"Is there anything to pay?" asked John.

"No sir, it's all been taken care of, just sign here and we will be on our way."

John signed the paper and the next moment the two young men were away.

Well, thought John, *there's a turn up for the book, fancy old Peter leaving me this chair. What I will do is give it a good clean.*

John set about cleaning and polishing the chair and when he had finished it looked a lot better. "Well, I suppose I will see how it feels to sit in it, now that it is clean."

As he sat down the chair's arms seemed to wrap around him and the high back wings held his head as a gentle woman would hold a child.

Oh yes, thought John, *I could spend hours in this chair.*

Suddenly he heard a voice say very quietly, "You will, John, you will."

John leapt out of the chair to see where the voice had come from, for he was certain he had heard a voice. He dismissed it, thinking he had probably only heard the noise because he was feeling so tired.

John looked at the chair, sat down once more, and felt that wonderful feeling of peace.

He closed his eyes and then he heard the voice once more. "Don't be alarmed, John, it's your chair that is talking to you. We will talk together whenever you wish; I assure you that you are not going mad!"

This time John did not move; he did not feel any threat from the chair, just complete peace.

"Go on, speak to me again," said John as if challenging the chair to answer back.

It did!

"Well John, let me try to explain to you who or what I am.

"I was made many years ago by a very wise man, who, through magical means, allowed me to have a spiritual soul, and to speak. I can only speak to the owner of the chair when he sits in it, provided that he is a good soul himself.

"I can help and advise him on all sorts of problems and can help his friends also, for I am bound to the owner of the chair if, as I said, that owner is someone of good intentions.

"My name is Trad and I'm called a listening chair. I suppose you would liken me to what you would call a counsellor in your world."

John was amazed, to say the least, by what a day this had turned out to be—a listening chair!

"Trad," he said, "do you read my thoughts? If I have a problem, do you give the best advice?"

"Yes and no, really—yes to other people's problems but not to your own," he replied, "and only if you are in the chair. At any other time I cannot. Your friend Peter was a very happy man when he died. He talked a lot to me about the time in the park when he first met you."

Just then a knock at his door brought John back to the reality of his world. Getting up, he could hear a scratching at the bottom of the door itself and his old friend Sam shouting, "Are you in, John? It's Sam here."

John opened the door and there stood Sam with his awful dog that snarled and snapped at everybody, including John.

"Hello Sam, what can I do for you?" asked John.

"John," said Sam, "I don't know what to do about my Freddy here."

"Come in, Sam, and tell me what's got you so up tight."

Sam came and sat down whilst John went to his new chair.

"That's a nice looking chair, John, I've never seen that in here before."

"Yes, it came today, an old friend left it to me and they brought it around this morning." *Better not say too much keeping about the chair's powers,* he thought. "Now Sam, what's up with your dog—our Freddy here?"

"Well, he seems as if the devil himself has got into him, he just will not do as he is told and really, it is getting on my nerves."

Now normally Freddy would have been barking and trying to bite up John's best slippers, but now he was sitting very quietly at John's feet.

"He must be sick," said John, "he and I don't normally get on well together, but look at him now!"

Sam could not believe it. John was right, yet only hour ago Freddy had been ready to take on the world.

Just then a voice spoke into John's mind. "You know what is wrong with the dog? It's lonely. It hasn't anybody to play with, especially another dog!"

John was by now getting used to Trad and so he said to Sam, "I think Freddy is lonely. Why don't you take him out more often? Probably a run in the woods would do. Why not also take him to training lessons; there he can be with other dogs."

Sam thought about this and did agree that Freddy had not been out very much of late, what with him not feeling up to running around with him at his age. "Okay," said Sam, "I will try it out to see if it has any effect on him."

John added, without thinking about it, "He'll be all right now, Sam, I have that feeling."

As Sam got up, the dog walked over to him and seemed to say, "It's time to go."

After Sam had left John sat down in the chair and asked if Freddy's sudden quietness was Trad's doing.

"Of course it was, how could you help anybody with a great dog growling at you? Also, I projected that thought to you to give to Sam so his dog will be a lot better from now on. Don't forget that other life forms can be 'out of sorts' just like humans."

"Well," said John, "I must get tidied up, I'm expecting a lady to call on me later. She is a widow and really she wants cheering up, so I'm cooking her a meal. If you don't mind, please don't intrude into my thoughts while she is here," said John with a laugh.

At seven, there came a knock on the door. John knew it was Susan because she was always on time. *I suppose I could get to know her better*, John thought, *she is a real friend indeed.*

"Hello Susan, come in, let me take your coat," said John.

Susan entered the old room and smelt the meal that was on the table. "Oh John, what a nice surprise—a meal for two," she said with a twinkle in her eye.

After the meal John invited her into his lounge and she saw the chair. "What's this then, John—new, isn't it?"

"Well yes," replied John, "and no. Sit down and I will tell you what has happened."

John told her all about what had occurred during the day, and about Freddy. She listened in raptures; she had always thought that John's voice was wonderful to listen to.

When John had finished she was just as amazed as he had been. "John, may I try the chair?" she asked.

"Go ahead, Susan, but I don't think it will work for you," said John.

Susan sat in the old chair. It felt very comfortable; she seemed to sink into it and a feeling of well-being came over her. She sat for a few moments listening for any form of sound, but none came.

"Well John, it feels very nice to sit in—a sort of a homely feeling—but you were right, not a word."

John asked her to let him sit in the chair and to ask him about something about which he had no knowledge. They changed places and he sat looking at her.

She started to say to him, "John, I have a friend whom I have been trying to help, somebody who you don't know who has got himself into a blind alley not knowing what to do, His name is—"

"His name is Paul," said John, interrupting her, "and he must tell the police all he saw. It will be all right in the end, as this Paul will get help to the old lady he saw taking the goods from the shop. The old lady he saw is doing it to draw attention to herself because she is lonely and has a great need for companionship."

Susan was taken aback, there was no way John could have known what her friend had seen, or even his name. "John, can you help anybody?" she asked.

"I suppose so, I don't know. You see, it wasn't me doing the talking, it was Trad—let me ask him."

The voice of Trad replied, "I seem to be able to help people most when they come to the sitter—

that's you, John—and when you help people, it is like a force feeding strength to me. This energy is like a life force that feeds my fibres."

Trad then asked, laughing, "What does Susan have in mind? Ask her."

John said, "I believe that I'm a sitter and I may be able to help most people, and this in turn enriches the life of Trad. Have you noticed that the chair is looking better?"

Susan then asked if it might be possible for her to bring a friend round tomorrow to see him. Her friend was very depressed, some form of illness, she believed.

John agreed to see the lady, but only if Susan was there also.

"All right," she agreed, and as she got up she gave John a great big hug. "You know, John," she said, "your friend has given you a wonderful gift, and I know you will use it wisely."

Susan thought it was wonderful; John was such a great companion. "John, I could stay all night here with you but I really have a lot to do. She gave John one more hug, saying, "Got to rush, got a lot to do, bye-bye," she called out as she swept through the door. "See you tomorrow!"

John sat back into the chair and pondered over what she had said. She was right, he had been given a wonderful gift. *I wonder if Trad can advise me how best to use this gift*, he thought.

Trad was listening to John's thoughts and replied, "John, I may be your chair now, but one of the things I cannot do is advise my owner! Yes,

John, my maker was a wise man, he made this chair to be a counsellor, not a judge.

"You, John, may listen to the advice I give you but it is up to you how you pass it on to help other people. I cannot help you with your own problems, as this would take away your ability to judge and you would not be able to think for yourself. You must decide how to use me. Rely on what your friend saw in you—I believe you call it a gut feeling?"

John knew he was right, and that night he wrestled with the problem of how to best use the chair. In the morning he was no nearer to an answer.

He was just about to sit down with his morning tea when he heard a loud banging on his door. He rushed to open it and there was Mrs White crying her eyes out.

"Oh Mr Cane," she sobbed, "I have been robbed, they have taken my old ring that my Sam gave to me many years ago!"

John sat her down and asked her if anything else was missing.

"No," she replied, "just my ring and it meant so much to me."

"Look, Mrs White," said John, "you may have lost it indoors. Calm down—a lady of your age must not get upset so!"

John sat in the chair and straight away Trad's voice said, "Tell her to look in the bottom of her knitting bag."

John looked at the old lady and said, "Have you looked everywhere? I seem to remember that two days ago you were doing some knitting—have you looked in your old knitting bag?" he asked her.

"Yes, of course I have, it's nowhere to be seen, it's gone forever," he said, sobbing her heart out.

"Come on, Mrs White," John comforted her, "we will both have another look around for it."

It was dark in the old lady's home, and he pretended to search over her whole place, gradually making his way to the knitting bag. "Let's look once more in here, shall we?" John said.

The old lady took out all her wools and laid them onto the table. John then turned the bag inside out, and there was not a sign of the ring.

"There, I told you so, it's gone!" Mrs White cried out in despair.

John then looked more closely at the balls of wool and there in the middle of one was a glitter, catching what light there was in the old lady's home. "Is this it, Mrs White?" asked John, picking the ball apart.

"Yes, that's it! Where was it?" she asked, jumping for joy. "You have found it, oh thank you, Mr Cane, how can I ever repay you?"

John said there was no need for payment, "just be happy and try putting the ring somewhere safer."

He left her sitting in her living room with a happy glow on her face. "Bye-bye, Mrs White, see you soon," he said as he left her.

Later that day Susan called round with her friend to see him. "This is Lily," said Susan, "the lady I was telling you about, John."

"Hallo," said John, "do come and sit down."

Lily looked at John and felt an immediate feeling

for him. His eyes seemed to radiate care and that feeling of inner trust. "Hallo John," she said, "it was so good of you to see me with such short notice, and me being a perfect stranger."

John sat Lily down next to Susan on the old settee. "I hope you don't mind, but I have asked Susan to stay with us whilst you tell me your problem," said John.

"No, of course I don't mind," she replied.

"Let me tell you something about myself," Lily started to say, "I am happily married to my Tom. Of late he has been really down on himself and no matter how hard I try, I cannot get him to snap out of it. It is really making me so sad to see him like this. I don't know which way to turn, I'm living on my nerves. He had a telephone call a few weeks ago and since then he has gone into himself, he won't tell me what it was all about, he just went deep into himself. It's driving me to despair," she said as she burst into tears.

"Now, now," said John, "it can't be as bad as that."

John sat opposite her in the chair and he heard Trad saying, "You have got to talk to him directly, as he is feeling really sad about an old friend of his. This is a special friend who Tom knew long before he met Lily. They used to do everything together and now he is dying.

"Will the pattern of their life continue, each experiencing what the other is? Tom is worried that he is going to die, as his friend is. I suggest that you persuade Lily to arrange a meeting; I will give you all the background on him in order to help him accept that what you tell him is the truth."

John turned to Lily and told her something of what Trad had said. She agreed that a visit would be good for her husband and that maybe next weekend he could stay the night, "along with Susan, if you are free," she said, turning to her friend.

It was all agreed that next Saturday would be best. After a cup of tea, Lily went home to make all the arrangements. Susan looked at John and said, "I do hope we can help her, I really hope we can."

Over the next few days Trad told John all about Tom, from the day he started to crawl to the day he met Lily. This was so that John could generate the confidence he would need to convince Tom that what he was telling him was true. Once he had Tom's trust John could then offer a solution to Tom's present problem.

Saturday came around very quickly. Susan came to collect John and away they went to see Tom and Lily.

"This should be a very interesting weekend, especially if you can help Tom," Susan said.

When they arrived it was Tom who came to the door. He seemed to be in a good mood.

Lily shouted down the hall, "Come in, come in, I've got the tea on so we can sit and have a good old chat."

The chat turned out to last well into the evening and with the knowledge Trad had given him, John was able to offer a solution to both their problems. "Now listen you two," said John, "will you both try something for me? I'd like you both to change roles for just one week."

"What?" said Tom. "You would like for me to do all the work Lily does for a week and for her to do all mine!"

They both looked at John and suddenly burst out laughing. "Oh John, you are a one," said Lilly, "but what an idea. You really mean that he should do all the things that I do and I do all that he does, or should be doing?"

"Yes," said John, "but only for a week, and if you don't know what to do then you must ask and the other must give a honest answer. Do you think you could do that?"

They both agreed that for the week they would switch responsibilities and would let him know how they got on. The rest of the weekend went well and John really enjoyed Susan's company. On Sunday evening they bade their farewells to Tom and Lily and said that they would see them in a week's time.

Driving back home John kept having an uneasy feeling that something was wrong, and it got stronger the closer he got to home. As he turned into his street he saw lorries parked outside his front gate. He quickly parked his car.

As he was about to enter his street door that led up to his flat a workman came out carrying a sack of rubble. "What's happened?" John asked.

"Well," said the workman, "I'm only the emergency staff, you understand, but the old lady upstairs apparently left the gas on when she went out yesterday to get her Saturday shopping and when she returned she found the fire engines putting out the fire that was caused by the gas explosion. They reckon that it was only an electrical fault but it has done a load of damage—it's lucky that nobody was at home at the time as the fire has not merely burnt her flat but all the others on that floor. We have been clearing out the flats as all that is left is smouldering. If you want more information you will have to see my boss, he is inside."

John raced upstairs and all he could see was the black charred remains of the landing. He went to where his door was and walked into what had been his home.

"Er, you can't go in there, it's somebody's place!" a voice called out.

"I can; I'm the somebody!" said John in a state of shock.

"Sorry sir, but you have to be careful because a house is still somebody's place even after it has been damaged. Luckily you weren't here, sir, because you most certainly would have been killed by the fire if not by the explosion."

"Where have they put all my furniture?" John asked, as the rooms had nothing in them.

"Well sir, as all the furniture was burnt it has been thrown onto the local tip and anything that survived the fire, like metal objects or items tucked away in cupboards, is being held by the council office for safe keeping."

John could only stare at what was left of his home. Susan, who had been trailing behind him the whole time, sensed how he was feeling and took charge, saying, "Now you will have to live with me. Well, at least until you have decided what you want to do."

Although she felt sad for him, she felt that at last she had the opportunity to make him happy, as that was all she had really wanted to do.

As they drove away he looked over his shoulder and knew that he would never again be as he had and, of course, he would never hear Trad again. Thank goodness he had Susan! Maybe it was meant to be and the fire had been the hand of fate, knocking him out of his set ways.

※※※※

Old man Peters was the first to notice the old burnt-out chair on the council tip and he asked his old mate Gerry if he could have it. He had been looking for an old seat for his allotment shed so that he could sit outside after doing some of planting.

Having been in the furniture business all his life, he felt he could restore the chair to its former condition. He took the burnt chair back with him in his old wheelbarrow and put it in the shed. *I will have a good look at tomorrow,* he thought to himself.

The next day he examined it closely and knew what he had to do. It seemed as if the chair understood what he was about to do, but of course that couldn't be, as it was just a chair!

Over the course of the next two months the chair

was transformed from an old burnt and charred frame into a beautifully restored piece. Peters stepped back to admire his work and thought, *Now for the test!*

He sat down in the chair and felt so peaceful. As he closed his eyes to really get the feeling of the chair a voice spoke to him and said, "Thank you."

Peters jumped up from the chair in surprise and said, "Who said that?" Nobody was around. He looked at the chair and thought he was going out of his mind. He then turned and sat down once more. He closed his eyes once more and the same voice said, "Don't be afraid, just sit still and I will explain everything to you..."

The listening chair was now alive once more.

The Seeing Stone

Young Tommy was walking on the beach; he loved the sea. There was something about the sea that seemed to attract him. It was unfortunate that this was to be the last day he would walk along his favourite beach—he had to get back home with his parents.

He was determined to keep the memories of what he had done. Here he was, ten years old—although he felt a lot older than his age—thoroughly enjoying playing in the sand amongst the pools at the edge of the shore.

He knew it was time to get back to the old house because by this time, they were probably hunting for him. His dad would have packed the car by now. He shuffled along the beach and up towards the footpath. As he went along, he aimlessly kicked the stones along the beach, and one stone in particular caught his eye. It seemed to wink at him. He bent down and picked the stone up.

I've found a marvellous stone here.

Ooh, he thought to himself, *I've found a marvellous stone here. I know what I'll do, I'll take it home and I'll polish it. Then, I'll always have it to remind me of my part of the beach.*

He put the stone into his pocket and, it being rather large, it made quite a bulge. He would have to hold it, because it would probably make a hole in his pocket. Running down the path over the sand dunes, the old house came into his view. He could see his mother there. "Come on, Tommy, come on—you're late!" she called to him.

Tommy stopped to take one last look. He wouldn't forget this place.

Mr and Mrs Kerr had always come down to the seaside with their boy Tommy, but this trip was special because they where going to move—they were going to live in France and this was to be the last time they would see their old sea shore. They both had memories themselves, particularly of how they had seen their Tommy grow up over the years, and now look at him—he was ten!

Tommy hurried up to his mother. "Are we ready to go then, Mum?" he asked.

"Yes Tommy," replied his mother. "Your dad's all packed and waiting in the car."

They got in the car and drove away.

Tommy sat back, thinking about the time when he was a boy, all those years ago. Now here he was in the Peak District in the middle of England with his own place now, and he loved it. He thought back to that last day again.

Whatever happened to that stone I picked up on the beach? he wondered to himself. *I know! I put it in the box, didn't I? That's it!*

With that, he jumped up from his chair and climbed up into the loft in search of his stone. He found the old box from years ago—it brought back sad memories of when he was in France. He had only been eighteen, doing his own thing as teenagers did, when he received the telegram informing him of his parents' death in an accident. Tommy was then the man of the house, and he had to deal with all the usual affairs. When it was over, he had returned to England.

He took the lid off the old tin box. The box had always been his prized possession because his father had given it to him to keep all his very own little bits in. Tucked in the corner was the stone that he'd found all those years ago. He sat and he held it in his hands. It felt good.

I never did get round to polishing this, did I? he thought to himself. *I think I'll have a go now.* He took the stone downstairs with him. It was very grubby, and it took all his might to polish it. Finally, the stone shone, almost like a piece of glass. As he held it up to the light, he swore he saw a shadow or something go across it.

That's daft, he thought to himself, *must be a trick*

of the light. He polished and polished some more, until his stone didn't seem like a humble stone anymore—it was more like a piece of quartz glass.

He lifted it up once more, then quickly dropped it—the shadows had moved. The shadows were moving, but they weren't shadows.

He turned the stone at different angles, and he could see a picture. He was stunned. He tried to work out what the picture was—it seemed almost like a video camera, with pictures you could see on a screen.

He could make people out—shapes—and then he stopped. He rushed to his drawers and pulled out a magnifying glass, holding it to the stone. The stone became very big under the magnifying glass. As he watched the picture, it was as though he was looking at a television set.

Tommy mounted his stone on a frame, securing his magnifying glass in front of it. He could see the pictures now very clearly. He couldn't understand what was happening; he had a stone, and he could see pictures in it. But what exactly was he seeing? As he continued to look at the stone, he saw things happening. Yes! He could see clearly! There was a procession, and he soon realised what it was.

The procession was the crowning of the queen.

This is impossible, he thought to himself. *This happened years ago!*

He watched in amazement. It was just as though he was watching a history programme on television—a recording of what had already been.

He picked up the frame and moved it. As it

moved, the picture changed. A clear image was now projected from the stone—it looked as though the stone was taking him back to around 1950. He could see someone on a mountain.

Then he remembered. Yes, the mountain! They conquered Everest in 1953. It was amazing. It appeared that as he turned the stone in different directions, so he could see different pictures from the same period in time.

He could see history; he could see it was the truth. It wasn't as though man had made a film and put in his interpretations, he was actually seeing history, the past, the way it really had been.

He began moving the frame about. He went back to the procession, then pulled the frame closer towards him. Gradually, the procession began to vanish. It appeared that the closer the frame and the stone were to him, the more modern the event he was seeing. He found he could adjust the frame according to the decade he wished to look at.

⋄⋄⋄⋄

He couldn't believe what he was seeing. There was the racing of the horses, the winners. He could see 1960, 1970, 1980 as he pulled the frame more towards him. Depending on what direction he chose, a different picture appeared.

He sat back, contemplating what he had found. He wondered why it should be him who had picked this particular stone out of the thousands on the beach.

Tommy put down the frame and the stone and went to make himself a cup of tea. He looked out across the moorlands of the Peak and thought about his seeing stone. Here he was with something that no one else in this world possessed.

He could see the past. He could challenge historians, for he could see the truth. He decided that he could even write a book about the history of the world, as seen through the seeing stone.

He put all things to one side. It seem as though the stone was drawing him to it. He looked at the stone in the frame, shining and bright.

Right, let's see how far back in history I can go, he thought to himself.

He adjusted the stone within the frame so that he could work out the year, the month, the week—the exact day he wished to view. He worked out the calibration, so he had direction and time. He chose carefully.

He chose several events from history, and looked at the stone. He saw what was happening, and made notes: who was doing what; how; which; where; and, more importantly, when. He was amazed.

Unsure about what to do with his findings, he put his notes together in a simple language, for he was not an historian, and sent them to a friend of his. He knew that this old friend used to study history at University. The days passed by and became weeks, and still he heard nothing from his friend. The following month, a letter arrived; it was from his friend Paul, the historian.

> *Dear Tommy.*
> *Thank you for this information you have given me—I never knew you were interested in history! What you have put down are some historical notes that only scholars would know about I'm fascinated to find out where you studied all this. Could you, do you think, write an article about a time in history and talk to us here at the University?*
> *Your old friend,*
> *Paul*

Tommy read the letter over and over again. Paul was a good friend of long standing. Tommy decided to pick the great fire of London as his topic—it was said that it had started at a certain time and certain place.

Tommy tuned in the frame to the 17th century and the year 1666. He saw the old streets of London, and he wrote down a detailed description of everything he saw.

When he had finished, he sat back. He knew he had the truth. He wondered if anyone would ever believe him. He sent off his notes to his friend Paul and, not within weeks but within days, he received an answer back. Paul asked Tommy to visit the university, which he did.

"How do you know this? Where have you studied

all this detail?" Paul asked Tommy as they sat together at the University. "It's almost as if you've actually been there, actually studied these occurrences."

Tommy smiled to himself. "Paul," he said, "lend me your ear." Tommy told Paul the whole story, beginning where he found the stone as a small boy and ending with his magnificent discovery.

Paul was absolutely amazed. He insisted on showing his learned professors what Tommy had uncovered. Paul asked Tommy whether he could see the stone. Tommy thought about this momentarily.

"Well," he said, "I haven't actually got it with me, but if you'd like to visit me, I'll gladly show it to you."

A lecture was arranged for him to show the professor his notes. By now, the news was buzzing around the university—who was this young historian who knew so many things? Tommy's name was spreading.

Paul took up Tommy's invitation and went and visited him. He was amazed by the way Tommy had set up the frame. "May I look at it?" Paul asked.

"Sure," replied Tommy, "help yourself."

Paul lifted the frame up to the light of day. All he could see was the sun shining through the stone. He turned to Tommy. "Er, I can't see anything, it's just like looking through a crystal. There's nothing there, Tommy."

Tommy picked up the frame and studied it himself. He could see the pictures. Then it dawned on him. The stone was meant for him only. "Paul," he said, "I can see it now. I can see it!"

"Hold on there," replied Paul, "I have an idea. Do you have a camera?"

"Yes," said Tommy, "I've got one upstairs. I'll fetch it."

Tommy returned with his camera, an old Instamatic.

Paul suggested that if Tommy could see the pictures, he should photograph them. Tommy agreed to try. He tuned in the frame and set up the camera, taking the shots. He took a picture of soldiers, soldiers in uniform like Grenadier Guards. They both waited for the pictures to develop. Still Paul could see nothing—the pictures came out blank. All they showed was an out-of-focus shot of the frame.

The stone was clear in the photos. Tommy sat back, considering this.

"Paul, I'm not mad, you know I'm not mad. It works."

"Don't worry, Tommy. What we'll do is an experiment, here and now. I know an awful lot about history, especially the period of Oliver Cromwell. I've seen documents that you haven't seen regarding Cromwell and some of his movements. Try me—try this, Tommy. Look at the period of 1642, and tell me about Cromwell."

Tommy picked up the frame and adjusted it so that he was right in tune with 1642. He described events happening then, events in Parliament, what Cromwell was doing, what he was saying. He wrote them down and handed the notes to Paul. Paul sat back and read the notes. He looked up in wonder.

"Tommy, it appears only you can do this. But what you have done is so marvellous—you can see anything."

Tommy and Paul thought about this for the next few days. Tommy was trying to understand why it should be him, him alone, who was allowed to see past events in the seeing stone.

While he was thinking, the newspaper was delivered. He saw the headline: *A CHILD IS LOST—POLICE SUSPECT FOUL PLAY."*

The child referred to in the article was a small four-year-old girl who had been missing for over a week. Tommy thought about this—he wondered if the seeing stone could possible help.

He looked at the date of the paper, mentally going back one week. He picked up the frame and scanned the areas the child might have been playing in, the areas where the papers said the child had last been seen.

He gasped. He could see the girl playing around the edge of a field. Suddenly a man came into the field, an oldish man with a serious expression. The man smiled at the girl and began talking to her.

She listened attentively, then they both climbed into the old man's blue car.

Desperately, Tommy tried to read the number plate. Persevering, he finally made out the letters and numbers. He wrote down all he had seen very quickly as the car gradually faded from his vision.

He tried to follow the car with his seeing stone

and as he moved, the picture changed. He put the stone down and realised what he had seen. He wondered whether anyone would believe his story. Tommy decided to visit the local police. He was sure they wouldn't believe him, but even so, he gave them the information he'd seen.

"Well sir, how do you come about this information then?" enquired the constable.

"Well, if I told you, you'd never believe me," replied Tommy. "Just put it down to the fact that I know."

The policeman took the information, and just to humour Tommy, ran the information through the computer. The vehicle licence number Tommy had given him was registered as a blue Ford car, with an owner fitting the description Tommy had given him.

Over the next few days the man was charged with kidnapping. The police had found the little girl at his home; the old man was mentally disturbed, having recently lost his own small granddaughter. He didn't want to hurt the little girl, he just wanted to play.

Shortly, it was all over the papers how this mystery man had helped the police. Tommy's name became very, very well known and his help was sought on many occasions. Each time he tried to help, and he was always able to so.

One day Tommy became too tired: this was all too much for him, his life was just not his own. It seemed as though everybody wanted the seeing stone—he had received many offers from people wanting to buy it and someone had even tried to steal it from him. The stone itself was part of his life, but Tommy knew he could not keep it. It was changing his life. He knew he had to do something.

The following day, Tommy got into his car with the stone and drove all the way down to the seashore, the same seashore he'd been to when he was ten years old. The stone was shining very brightly. He looked at it.

"My old friend, you are too much for me. I cannot take the responsibility you have laid upon me. You are changing my life."

With that, he took the stone and threw it as far as he could out to sea.

The stone fell into the water and sunk to the bottom, awaiting to be rediscovered another day, another time, by another ten-year-old boy.

Panda Ling

Many years ago, to the far north in the ancient land of China, there was a massive forest. A very old woman called Loo Chun had lived alone in this forest since she was very young.

She depended on wild fruit and nuts for most of her food, trapping rabbits and small deer for an occasional meal of meat and using their skins for clothing. There was a time when she was young and pretty that a young man had been the apple of her eye, but that is another story.

A few years past a distant relative whom she had long forgotten had died, leaving behind a small baby girl called Ling. The elders of the village where Ling had been born had come across great difficulty in finding any member of her family to care for her, and only after much hardship had been able to identify and locate Loo Chun.

Great White Bear slowly entered the den

She, when first approached, was most unwilling to accept responsibility for the child and it was with considerable resentment towards authority that she took Ling into her simple home.

Ling turned six years old. Although Loo Chun had explained age and birthdays to the child, there were no presents or special treats for the little girl, and no other children to help make the day any different from any other in her lonely existence.

✧✦✧✦

Having eaten a simple breakfast, Ling asked Loo Chun, "May I go into the forest today? I promise I will keep out of your way. I could have a picnic in my special place, couldn't I Gran, please?" she pleaded.

"Oh all right," replied Loo Chun, only too pleased to get the little girl out from underneath her feet. "I'll pack you a basket, but stay within shouting distance. I don't want you getting lost so I have to waste my time looking for you. Make sure you put your cape on.

"Yes, Grandmother," Ling replied. She had been taught to address Loo Chun so although the relationship was in reality much more distant. The girl went to get her cape whilst a basket was made up for her.

As Ling prepared to leave Loo Chun said, "While you are out playing you can gather some of those red berries I showed you but don't go far. Do you understand, girl?"

"Of course I understand, Grandma," said Ling and left quickly before her Loo Chun could think of anything else for her to do.

Although she was only six, Ling had never liked the old woman; she had never been made to feel wanted or given the love with which most little children are raised by their parents.

She had a vague memory of a time when she had been happy, but perhaps this was only a childish dream. Today, as she walked along the forest path, she thought to herself, *One day I will leave and never come back, and then she'll be sorry!*

Such thoughts might have spoiled the pleasure to be had from a bright sunny day. The forest had always been a playground for little Ling and, once she was away from the doleful influence of the old woman, it seemed as though all things were possible.

She weaved her way down the old path, past her favourite tree—her wishing tree, she called it—where on many occasions she had wished and wished that things would change.

On, further, deeper into the forest she went and then down to the little stream. There, as she sat down on a log, an old friend she called Boo—a little rabbit—came across to her.

Boo had seen Ling many times in the past and had come to know her as a friend. Of course people and rabbits do not speak the same language, but Ling used to talk to her little friend and seemed to sense what the little rabbit thought, even without any words given in reply.

"Hello," said Boo, "what are you doing today? You look happy with yourself."

"I'm out enjoying myself all day—think of that, all day to myself!" Ling said and went on to tell her friend how her day had started and that it was her birthday.

"How wonderful!" Boo did a little jig. "So today is special! What are you going to do to celebrate?" he asked.

"Well, I'm going deeper into the forest today, to see things I have never seen before," she said, and with that she picked up her basket and waved farewell to Boo, promising to see him again soon.

As she went on, the trees seem to get bigger so that in some places the forest was so thick that very little sunlight came through the leaves, making it very hard to see.

This did not worry Ling too much. She felt so at home in the forest, and today was her birthday—a time for adventure.

She started to run in and out of the trees, laughing aloud, then suddenly she turned sharply and heard the sound of something tearing. She looked back and saw that her cape had caught on a bush and had torn in half. *Oh dear,* she thought, *now I will be in trouble with Grandma, she will hit me even if it is my birthday! I never want to go home ever again.*

Little did she know that what she had said was nearer to the truth than she realised.

As the hours passed, the forest got darker. Looking around, Ling came to realise that she had lost her sense of direction and that she was lost. In the light of the day she could have made her way home, but as darkness fell, everything seemed to close in on her.

She started to feel tired and crept under a bush, closed her eyes, and in no time at all, she fell asleep.

Now in this forest there lived a tribe of white bears, which few people had ever seen.

Two of these bears were walking nearby and one suddenly said to the other, "Look, over there under that bush—isn't that a small girl-person?"

The other bear looked in that direction and agreed with his friend. "What are we going to do? She can't be left here all night! I know, I will fetch Great White Bear and see what he has to say."

So off went one of the bears whilst the other stood watch over Ling. In what seemed to be no time at all, the other returned with Great White Bear, who was the chief of the bear tribe.

"Well, what have we here now—a little girl, fast asleep?" the Great White Bear exclaimed.

Great White Bear knew that he could not leave her in the forest safely, so very gently he lifted her up in his great arms and carried her deeper and deeper into the forest, to a place where no man had ever been.

There, in a forest clearing, was a great den and many smaller dens that made up the bear village. Selecting one of the smallest dwellings, the Great White Bear carried the sleeping child into it and placed her, still fast asleep, on a bed of moss and leaves.

"I will decide what to do about her in the morning," said Great White Bear and went away, leaving one of the bears who had found her to keep watch over her as she slept.

Ling woke the next morning to the sounds of the birds singing outside and loud snoring from the corner of the den.

As she woke she looked around her and thought, *This wasn't where I feel asleep last night, where am I?* Looking round, she saw the little white bear, fast asleep! *Maybe I'm dreaming!* she thought, but just then the bear stirred, gave a small growl, and sat up suddenly.

Ling jumped back in surprise but curiosity soon overcame her nervousness. The little white bear saw that Ling was watching him and said, "Don't be frightened of me, my name is Chi."

"A talking bear! Now I must be dreaming—how can a bear talk to me except in a dream?"

Before she could say anything more, Chi went on to explain that he and the other members of his tribe were not like ordinary bears, but could read other people's thoughts. "Last night you were found under a bush, lost and cold in the forest, and we brought you here so that you would be safe until morning."

Ling was fascinated by Chi and the more he talked, the more she wanted to be with him. "Chi," she asked, "what is going to happen to me now that you have brought me here?"

"That's up to Great White Bear: he is old and wise and only he can decide what's to be done with you. Now you stay here while I go to fetch him."

At that, Chi ran out of the hut and down the path to the biggest den. He saw Great White Bear standing at his door, yawning and stretching, and told him that the girl was awake.

"Go and get her some fruit for her breakfast. I will see her now."

As Great White Bear slowly entered the den in which she had spent the night, Ling looked up at him in awe. He seemed enormous, so much bigger than anybody else she had ever seen in her life.

"Don't be afraid, Ling, I will not hurt you. My name is Gi, although my tribe address me as Great White Bear as a mark of respect. It is my job to look after everybody. Will you come out so that we can talk—your little hut is a bit too small for me."

"How do you know my name?" asked Ling, sitting on a log outside the hut.

"Well, as you now realise, we can talk to you as if by magic and I can read what's on your mind, so to speak."

Ling felt very happy, perhaps for the first time in her life, and suddenly all she wanted to do was to stay here forever and ever. Gi understood what she was feeling and knew that she did not want to go back home to live in sadness.

"Ling, won't your grandma be worried about you? You have been missing for twenty-four hours now!"

"No, she doesn't love me, that's why I wanted to run away! Can I stay? Please Gi, let me stay!"

Gi thought kindly about this little girl who loved the forest and seemed so gentle and caring. He then said to Ling, "This is what I've decided to do: I will send word to the area where you lived and find out what your grandma is doing about your loss. The news I get back will help me decide what I am going to do about you."

So Great White Bear's questions were passed from animal to animal through the forest and, before many hours had passed, a picture of the past events came back to him. He told Ling to sit down and listen to what he had to say.

"Ling," he started, "your grandmother, Loo Chun, who is really your great aunt, did not report you missing until nightfall. Many people went out looking for you during the night using lanterns, but all they found was part of your cape. This has led everybody to believe that you have been eaten by a wild animal and that you are dead.

"Your grandmother almost seems pleased that you are not with her anymore, although she is pretending to be sad about your death.

"I cannot let you go back and go through all that again. I propose that you grow up as a member of our tribe. Although you are not a bear and are so very different in many ways, you will obey our laws until you are eighteen years of age, when you will then be regarded as an adult. At that time you must start to look after yourself and move out of the forest to live.

"To help you get used to our way of life, I am asking Chi to be your companion and guide; he can look after you like a brother and a friend. Remember to let him teach you our ways. Now go and eat."

Ling jumped for joy and promised that she would never ever give Ci any cause to be angry with her. Great White Bear walked off into the forest with a thoughtful smile on his grizzled face.

Ling rushed off to find Chi and tell him all the news, but of course he already knew.

As the days rolled into months and the months rolled into years, Ling came to love all the white bears as if they were her own family, which in fact they had become. She learnt of their ways, traditions, and crafts.

One day when she was fifteen she asked Chi a question. "Chi, tell me, ever since I've known you, you have always chewed on a long stick—why?"

Chi showed her a stick and said, "Look at it. We find that it is very good for us and, as it is hollow, we can get our claws around it to hold easily."

Ling picked up the stick, looked at it, and saw how hollow it was. As she looked at it she seemed to recall seeing something like its many years ago, something that made a sound if wind was blown across or down it. She twirled the hollow stick around in a circle with the stick up high and, sure enough, a sound came out of the stick.

The following day Ling went off alone into the forest and as time went by, the bears started to wonder what was keeping her away for so long. As the evening shadows started to lengthen, Ling came back with a broad smile on her face and Chi asked her what she had been doing. "I'm picking up strange thoughts from you and so has everybody else!" he said.

"Wait until tomorrow and I will show you something," said Ling.

Nobody could wait for tomorrow and the dawn was little more than a glimmer on the horizon when the bears started to assemble in the large clearing. By then, nearly everybody had heard that Ling was going to do something special. Even Great White Bear had heard!

After she had had her morning drink, Ling took her place upon the large stone in the centre of the large clearing, her special place. Slowly she took the stick to her mouth and gently blew. She had made some holes in it, and when she placed her fingers on these holes and blew, a sound came out of the stick like no other sound that had ever been heard in the forest before.

It sounded like the trees singing and the music drifted from tree to tree throughout the forest.

She sat for nearly two hours playing, her audience listening with rapt attention. When at last she had finished, she said, "Each of you has given me something over the years I have been with you and now I am able to give you something in return. I will play for you, and those of you who would like to learn will be taught to play."

Great White Bear was happy for her and came up to her and hugged her (very gently, of course). "Ling," he said, "we all love you and thank you for your gift."

Everybody cheered and they all wanted to learn

how to play. Over the next few months Ling showed them, but none could alter the notes as their claws would not fit over the holes. All continued to listen to her concerts, as they found her music so beautiful.

One day Ling and her friends went off for a picnic, into a part of the forest that she had not visited before. After travelling for some hours they came to a spot that looked ideal, so they sat down to rest and to have their food. After eating, they all shouted for Ling to come and play with them, something which she had always enjoyed. "Come on," said Ling, "let's play chase! I'll go first."

Off went Ling as fast as she could, but not so fast that they could not keep up with her. "Here I am," she shouted from a bush but as she turned to continue her game she slipped and went tumbling down a steep slope.

The bears caught up, yelling, "Ling, where are you?" They could not see her.

Then one of the bears parted the bush and saw Ling at the bottom of the slope. "Over here, everybody, Ling is down here! Quick, we must help her!"

The bears scrambled down to where Ling laid so still. The bears wondered what to do; their Ling was hurt.

One of the bears said that he would go and get Great White Bear, as he would know what must be done. So the bear raced home and fetched the chief. He came back and, looking at Ling's body, knew that she was dead.

He felt a great sadness come over him, as he had come to regard Ling as his own granddaughter.

"We must get her back home and I will tell you all what to do next."

They gently lifted Ling's body up and took her home and laid her on her own bed. "What do we do now, Great White Bear, tell us!" they asked.

"Well, I've heard that when people die, they are placed upon a great fire so that their spirits may rise from them in the smoke," he said. "Their spirits then go to a place called heaven," he went on to tell them, "where they are very happy forever. This is the custom of Ling's people. We must make a great fire in honour of our Ling so that she may be happy also."

So a great fire was built and Ling's body was placed upon it and everybody gathered around as Great White Bear lit it.

The flames grew bigger and bigger and soon all what was left was a pile of ashes.

Great White Bear then stepped forward and said to everyone: "I want you to take these ashes and scatter them throughout the forest so that the forest will have something of Ling for ever more."

So, as the ashes cooled, all the bears took a small portion of it to many different parts of the forest. As they did so they hugged each other in sadness at the loss of Ling.

When they had finished they looked at each other and they saw that the ashes had turned some of their fur black, their eyes black where they had been crying, their arms black where they had been hugging, and their legs black where they had been rubbing.

Great White Bear saw this and declared that it was a sign of a new beginning .He declared that the whole tribe should, from that day forth, be known as panda bears and that Ling should always be known as panda Ling.

They all agreed and said they would from that day forward try and learn to play the sticks as Panda Ling had.

This is why, even today, the panda will so often be seen eating bamboo sticks; they are not eating them really, but trying to play them in memory of their panda Ling.

The Gift

It was Jane's eighteenth birthday, a day she decided to share with her grandmother. She would go round to see her in the afternoon. Ever since she could remember, her grandmother had always been there for her, taking the place of her parents who had died in an accident when she was just a baby. Jane had also been in the accident and people said it was a miracle she had survived.

When she had first started school it was Gran who had helped to ease the pain of going. She explained the need of schooling and helped Jane to see it as a great adventure. As she grew up, her grandmother had done as much as she could for Jane, letting her have her freedom to see life and yet keeping a watchful eye upon her.

During her early teens, Jane's grandmother had helped her through her first love affair. Looking back now, Jane laughed to herself to think what a

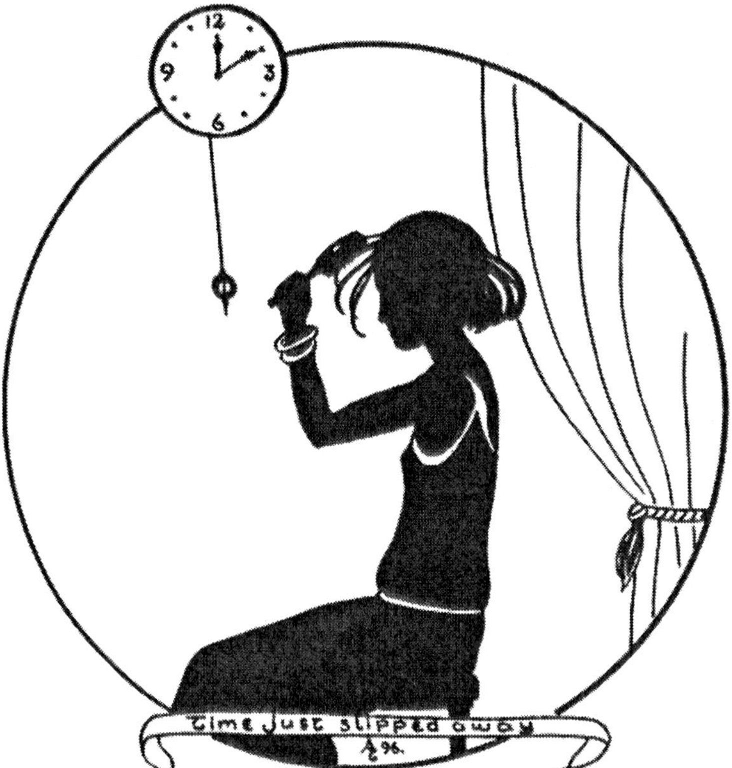
Time Just slipped away

fool she had been and how right Gran had been in her advice.

The most striking thing about her grandmother, something Jane would always remember, was her hair.

All of Jane's life her grandmother's hair had been beautiful. She used to tell Jane, "Your hair is like your life, if you do not keep it in order you will finish up with it all knotted."

Looking back, it seemed that whenever Gran had needed to think deeply about something or needed to make a decision, out came the old hair brush.

Jane had asked her once, when she was younger, "Gran, why is it that you always brush your hair whenever you are thinking about something? I have never seen you without your brush, it must be very old."

"Well, when you are older—and only I will know when the time has come—I will tell you all about my old brush," she said with that all-knowing smile she had.

That had been a few years ago when Jane had asked that, but there had been times in the past when Jane was ill when her grandmother would show her love for her by gently brushing Jane's hair with her hairbrush, a great honour indeed.

When Jane had turned seventeen she found a place for herself down the road from her grandmother's house. At first Jane did not want to move, but her grandmother had insisted that it was time that Jane learned to manage independently. To Jane it was a strange feeling at first—the guilt of leaving her Gran all alone mixed with the feeling of freedom growing greater.

Jane's first worries were soon dispelled by the arrival of Mrs Mackay, a retired nurse, whom her grandmother had known for many years.

They got on with each other like sisters. Mrs Mackay was firm with the old lady and yet very kind, as Gran, now in her seventies, had need for some help and extra attention.

The two of them used to talk and talk about this and that, putting the world to rights, and so when Gran suggested that it was time for Jane to spread her wings, her granddaughter knew that she had thought it out long before telling Jane!

One day, Jane was browsing in an old shop when she saw a little sugar bowl and thought that it would be a wonderful gift for her gran's birthday. As she walked in through the front door, she could hear Mrs Mackay chattering to Gran. "Hallo," she said, "look who has come to see you."

Gran turned in her chair and saw Jane, and a smile came over her face. "What a wonderful surprise to see you, Jane, come and sit down here next to me."

Jane came over to her and gave her a big hug. "Happy birthday, Gran, I've brought a little something for you."

"Oh Jane, you shouldn't have." As Gran undid the gift Mrs Mackay poured Jane a cup of tea. Gran's eyes lit up when she saw the gift and she said that she knew exactly where she was going to display it.

Gran then described all that had happened since she had last seen Jane; events that, although they seemed trivial to Jane, were matters of great importance in Gran's world.

Jane listened and then Gran looked at her in a way Jane had never seen before.

"Listen Jane," she said, "I want to tell you something that has been on my mind for a long time."

Mrs Mackay started to get up to leave the two to talk. She felt this was something private between grandmother and granddaughter.

"It's all right, Mrs Mackay," Gran said, "you don't have to get up; I would like you to listen to this."

"Jane," said Gran, "could you please go and get that old hairbrush down from my dressing table for me?" Jane looked at her gran and wondered what this was all about, but she did as she was bid.

"Many years ago, Jane," Gran said, holding the old brush, "this was given to me by my Gran, who had been given it by her Gran before her. When I was a child, my grandmother told me that this brush had a magic all its own.

"I was about your age, Jane, and you can understand that I looked at her in a funny sort of way, just as you are looking at me now," she said, smiling.

She went on to tell the story just as she had herself heard it many years before.

"Have you noticed how animals calm themselves by smoothing down their fur? Well, this brush does the same for me and, funny as it may seem, it works! Whether it is magic or not, the brush seems to know exactly how I feel and when I use it, ideas come into my mind that turn out to be the answers to nearly all my problems, no matter what they are."

Jane was fascinated by the story, as she was now beginning to understand why she had seen her Gran so often with the brush in her hand. Was it magic? She continued to ponder this question, because her Gran had always seemed to know the answers to help her.

Her gran continued with the story. "When the brush was first given to me, it felt so ordinary. As time went on it seemed to be that we got to know each other. When I used the brush it felt as though somebody was close to me, and yet nobody was there. At no time did I feel afraid—in fact it was like having a friend always there whenever I needed one.

"Eventually, I decided to call this friend by name, as it was better than speaking to it as if it was an inanimate thing. The name I chose was Simon, as I felt the friendly presence to be that of a man.

"Over the years he has guided me on many occasions and his advice has always proved to be well founded. He has never interfered with my personal life, yet he was always there when I needed him.

"I often wondered how all of this came about, as my Gran had said that there was a story, passed down from generation to generation through the family, that many hundreds of years ago the family knew an old man who was rather like a modern doctor, although the family believed him to have been a wizard.

"During his lifetime he had always loved one of the family, a girl called Jane. He would do anything for Jane and on her twenty-first birthday he gave her a hair brush and told her that whenever she had a need of him, she should just hold the brush to her hair and he would be there with her.

"When the old man was dying, all those years ago, he called for Jane and reminded her that whenever she was troubled, she had only to reach for the brush and he would be at her side. He went on to say that as he looked upon her as a grandchild, she must only pass the brush on to a grandchild when her time came.

"Over the years I have tried to ask Simon if the story about the old man is true. All I have ever got is a feeling of somebody smiling at me, so I have never gone further than that, but today, as it is your birthday, I'm passing this brush on to you. May Simon be with you also."

Jane took the brush from her grandmother, thanking her for the wonderful gift and the account of its history. About half an hour later, Jane said goodbye to her grandmother and set off home with her gift.

When she got in, she sat down and thought about what had happened so far that day. She picked up the brush to look more closely at it. Besides looking old, it seemed just like an ordinary brush. There were a lot of funny symbols on the backplate of the brush and as she held it, it did have that funny feeling about it.

She started to comb her hair and immediately

had an image of a cat being stroked. She could feel the way the way the cat felt: it felt so relaxing. As she continued to brush her hair she felt so much at ease that time just slipped away. After what seemed no more than a few moments, she put the brush down and realised that she had been stroking her hair for over an hour! *This will never do,* she said to herself, *I have to get ready to meet David soon.*

David was a friend she had been spending time with over the past few months. She felt that she was getting close to him and hoped that he was feeling the same towards her.

Tonight, he had asked her out for something special and she was looking forward to it very much. They seemed to have so much in common that she felt life without him would be very quiet.

The night turned out to be a very special one indeed. David asked her to marry him, and she agreed.

Over the next few months they worked together on all the arrangements for the great day and for their honeymoon. On the wedding day they felt so happy, as if the world was their playground. They were so tired that when they got on the aircraft to fly away on honeymoon, they fell asleep for most of the trip!

After ten days of the most romantic time of Jane's life, David got up early one morning, saying that he would like to climb the old rock face just outside the village. "Hope you don't mind," he said, "as I know that you don't like heights. I will take some pictures for you to see."

As he went into the bathroom, Jane got out of the bed and sat down at the dressing table. She picked up her brush and started to brush her hair. She felt him come up behind her, and he kissed her on her neck. "You look so beautiful as you brush your hair—I noticed that you brought your old brush with you!"

She looked up at him and said, "One day I will tell you about this old brush." She laughed. "Go on, go and climb your rocks but don't forget that we are going out tonight, you're just a young boy at heart!"

During the day she found so many things she had to do before getting ready to come home; last-minute gifts and making sure of all the travel arrangements. After a few hours she stopped for a drink and sat down to think about all that had happen to her since her grandmother had given her the old brush, as David had called it.

Once more she was drawn to hold the brush, it felt good. She wanted to brush her hair, to see if Simon was still around. Everything was all quite, an eerie silence. Suddenly there was a knock at the front door and there stood the local policeman. "Yes," she said, "what can I do for you? Do come in."

"Is your name Mrs Jason?" he asked.

She had to think for a second as she was still getting used to her new married name. "Yes, that's right, has something happened?"

"Well, there has been a nasty accident and your husband has been rushed to the hospital. I can run you down there if you wish, and on the way I can tell you what I know of what happened."

The doctor was waiting for Jane; his face told the sad story. "It appears that he was trying to climb down a cliff edge when he fell. It looks as though his back is broken, but I'm arranging for another doctor to see him," he said.

"Tell me," said Jane, "will he be all right?"

The doctor looked straight at Jane and said, "He is paralysed from the waist down and will never walk again, I'm sorry to have to tell you. If you would like to see him, he is awake. I have told him just what I have told you."

David was lying down on the bed with his eyes closed, his face covered in cuts and scratches. She bent over to kiss him and as with the sleeping princess, as she kissed him his eyes opened. He smiled up at her and said, "Sorry about this, darling, but it looks like I've ruined our honeymoon."

His eyes sparkled as he spoke and in that moment of time she loved him more than anything else in the world. "Don't worry, we have each other and that is what really counts, David."

After an hour or so, she said she had to go back to get things organised to get them back home. When she got back to the hotel she sat down in front of the dressing table mirror and then the shock hit her.

She cried and cried until there wasn't a tear left. "Come on, Jane my girl," she said to herself, "there's a thousand and one things you have to do and you look a mess."

She picked up her brush and started to brush her

hair. As she did so she started to feel relaxed, and then the voice of Simon came gently into her mind. "Jane, what has happened today has happened but all is not lost, you are going to have a family even though David cannot give you any more children."

"What do you mean, any more children, we haven't got any now," said Jane.

"Trust me," said Simon, "all is not lost."

Jane was in no mood to talk to Simon anymore and so she put the brush down and started to get on with all the arrangements for getting home.

Days turned into weeks and soon two months had passed since David's accident. Jane had been feeling run down and so had booked herself to see the local doctor, a Dr Javis.

He had been up to see David quite a few times and they seemed to be on friendly terms. He opened the great old surgery door and said, "Come in, Jane, I've found out what is wrong with you—you are pregnant, young lady!"

"But how can I be? David has been paralysed since our honeymoon and that was it."

"Well, all I can say is that just before the accident you and David did make love, and now you can see the results of it. I'm very happy for you both."

They just could not believe that they were going to have a child. "Are you sure there isn't any mistake," David asked, "you are really pregnant?"

"Yes of course I'm sure, I am so happy," said Jane.

Later that night, just before Jane got into bed, she reached out for the brush to do her hair. The familiar feeling of peace came over her and then she heard the voice of Simon. "Well, are you happy now, Jane? I told you to trust me. I will let you into another secret—your baby will be a girl and you will name her Mary."

"How do you know all this then, Simon?" asked Jane.

"Well Jane, I see many things and have many magical ways, as I'm the spirit of the brush. Would you wish me to tell you of the life Mary is going to have?"

"Not now, Simon, maybe at a later date. Leave me a little mystery in the life of a child who's not even born yet," said Jane.

"All right, when you wish," said Simon.

Once more Jane felt the comfort of Simon around her. She did not love Simon as she loved her David, for David was her life. Simon had become her special friend who she could talk to about her inner thoughts. Her grandmother had been right about how the gift of the brush would help. Simon was the brush and he was the gift.

The months flew past and at the end of July their daughter arrived. As Jane lay in bed with David next to her, she asked him what name should be given to the child.

"I would like to call her Mary, as she looks so saintly laying there," David replied.

Jane just smiled and agreed that Mary it should be. After the christening, when everybody had left and Mary was tucked up in her cot, Jane reached across for her brush. "Well Simon, what do you think of our Mary, isn't she beautiful?"

"Oh yes," said the gentle voice of Simon, "and her life will be full of adventures, some you will like and others you won't like," said Simon.

※※※※※

Jane sat back in her old armchair, thinking about her life and all that had happened since Mary had arrived in her life, over twenty years ago. David had died and all she had left was her Mary, and of course Simon. Soon Mary would be having her twenty-first birthday!

I will give her a special surprise on that day, thought Jane. *In fact, I will have to get organised as the big day is next week!*

That night she sat down to brush her hair and there was Simon in her thoughts. "So, you have no idea as to what you want to do for her," he said, reading her thoughts.

"Well, what do you suggest, Simon? It has got to be something very special that she will remember for the rest of her life."

Simon said very quietly to her, "Well, she is a woman now and she hasn't travelled at all, so how about treating her to a world cruise?"

"What!" she almost screamed. "My baby away for so long—I could not bear it!"

Simon calmed her down and told her about the wonderful adventure Mary would have, and how she would remember the trip for a very long time.

Jane thought about this and realised that in fact she was being selfish in wanting to keep her daughter at her side. In the end she knew that Simon was right, as he always was, and so she decided that first thing in the morning she would get the trip organised.

The party was a great success. The evening went on and Jane watched her Mary dancing with every young man, and it brought back memories of when she was younger.

When the music stopped Mary looked across to her mother and smiled. She knew that when the time was right her mother would let her know what she had done for her birthday.

"Mary," Jane called to her daughter, "come over here, I've got something for you."

Here we go, I wonder what it is: she has never forgotten my birthday, Mary thought with excitement as she approached her mother. "Oh mum, this is a wonderful party, thank you so much—what a wonderful present!"

"Mary," said Jane, "the party is not my present to you—but this is." She handed Mary a package and watched as she unwrapped it. Inside the package were all the details of the trip around the world Jane had planned for Mary.

Mary stood amazed; she could not believe her eyes. "Mum, what can I say, you must have been reading my mind. I was starting to save up for a trip abroad and I was wondering how to tell you about it. You are the best mum in the world!"

The rest of the party was a blur, all she could talk

about was her forthcoming trip around the world. She was a child once more and yet not a child but a woman. Jane's baby had grown up.

Over the next month Mary flew around making all the final arrangements for the trip, for she had decided that the trip would take a year in all, as she planned to stop here and there on the trip to see the sights.

Jane wasn't too happy, but it was what Mary wanted to do and of course Simon was all for it. She often wondered if Simon was more on Mary's side than hers, but she had to admit that in the end Simon was right.

The day of departure came and Jane still had a funny feeling that she would not see her daughter again, but she put this down to the sadness of not seeing Mary again for over a year.

"Don't worry, Mum, I will write to you," Mary called back as she went into the departure lounge.

Then she was gone.

Jane left the airport quickly and, with a heavy heart, returned home, filled with a deep foreboding that she would never see Mary again.

That night, as Jane brushed her hair, Simon came into her mind. "Listen to me, I know that you are sad about her trip, but she is young and in today's world, she has to find herself."

"I know that you are right, but it doesn't help how I feel. I have a feeling I am losing her and I can't shake it off. Do you know something that I do not, Simon?"

"In our lifetimes we go through many phases.

This is the just the start of one phase in your lifetime. Just leave it at that and trust me."

Over the next few months the postcards began to arrive, all saying how wonderful life was. It seemed Mary had no time to write a letter, just a quick scribble here and there. *Well, at least she is still in touch with me,* Jane thought, *and my Simon is always here at my side if doubts creep in.*

Simon told her to get out and about more, for there was more in life than just her daughter. "I will always be with you, so enrich your days," he said. Jane decided to help with the local village voluntary group and it did help the time to pass.

It had been a year since Mary had gone away, on the day the letter arrived. Jane sat down and read it slowly.

> *Dear Mum,*
> *I have met this wonderful man and he wants me to marry him.*
> *I know I haven't been back since I left last year, but life has been so good that it seems as if time does not exist. Can I bring him home to meet you, so you can judge for yourself? I will not go into all that's happened, so that you can talk to Peter yourself—yes, his name is Peter. Please ring me at the above number and I will arrange everything.*
>
> *Lots of love,*
> *Mary*

So my little Mary is getting married, Jane thought. *I bet Simon knew all about this, he always seems to know what was going to happen.*

All her life, from the day her grandmother had given her the brush, he had been a part of her life. *One day I will pass the brush onto my granddaughter*, she thought, *and I hope he will look after her as he has me—that's if I do have a granddaughter!*

That night Jane thought all about that had happened since she had been given the gift of the brush. She thought about the brush's history, as told to her by her grandmother, and how she in turn would have to tell the story to her granddaughter.

What would happen if she did not pass the brush on? What would happen to Simon? Only one person could set her mind to rest and that was Simon himself.

She picked up the brush and started to brush her hair. As she relaxed Simon started to speak to her. "It seems as if your family is asking questions and I'm always trying to answer them, but let's start with yours first," he said. "Your family has always had a sense of tradition and you are no exception. You will be passing on your gift as it has been done in the past. That is why I have been with you all for so many years.

"When I was created many hundreds of years ago by your ancestors through a magical act, it was built into my existence that I would help my owner to enable me to exist.

"So over the years I have become, as you might

say, part of the family, even if I am only connected to one member of the family at a time. One of the many magical acts protects grandchildren from outsiders, and your ancestor gave them a gift that would be with them from when they were eighteen years old until they could pass the gift on, directly or indirectly.

"I have been left twice in the past by deed of covenant in a will, and all that time I have helped my owners to solve their problems. You yourself have, I hope, felt this during your lifetime.

"I have been like a personal counsellor in times of stress. Once you have passed the gift on the rest of your life will be peaceful until you die.

"Before you ask what's on your mind, know that I'm not permitted to tell you when you will die. It is a law of the magical rite."

Jane sat back and listened to the history of the gift as Simon went on to explain that after she passed on the gift, she would see Simon for the first time in her life since her grandmother had given her the brush when she was eighteen years old.

It was funny, but she could not think of Simon as a gift, he had been part of her life for so long.

She started to think, *Will I give this gift to my unborn grandchild? What would I say to her? This is something Simon can not help me with, but when the time comes I feel I will know what to say.*

Suddenly she started to feel very tired and she told Simon that she would lay down for a while. As her head touched the pillow, she feel into a deep sleep.

"Gran, are you all right?" said a voice in Jane's conscious mind.

"What—who are you," Jane asked, trying hard to get all her senses back.

"Oh Gran," said the young girl, "you are always playing jokes on me. I'm Dorothy, your granddaughter, and you asked me to give you a shake in time for tea."

Jane looked at the girl and thought herself still asleep—she had to be dreaming. She looked at the girl and could see that she was in fact awake. *What has happened to all the years?* Jane thought. *Am I going out of my mind?*

"Don't forget about the party tonight, Gran, we are going to enjoy ourselves—after all, it's not very often a gran and her granddaughter have the same birthday."

A birthday party—mine or hers? How old am I? she thought to herself as Dorothy left the room.

Jane looked around her bedroom. It did not seem to have changed. She got off the bed and made her way towards her dressing table. There on the table top was a birthday card. It read, "Happy birthday Gran, on your 70th birthday. Love, Dorothy."

So now I know how old I am—seventy! she thought. As she put the card down she saw the brush and she remembered Simon. She picked up the brush and started to brush her hair.

Simon's voice spoke to her once more. "Hello Jane, so you are with us."

Jane asked Simon what had happened to her. It seemed as if time had slipped past so quickly, eighteen years had just gone in a flash.

"Well," said Simon, "you simply got into so a deep thinking session about what would happen in the years to come, that you just went into your own world, blocking out your real self, including me," said Simon laughingly. "So now it is your granddaughter's eighteenth birthday, I wonder what you have got her as a present?"

My goodness, thought Jane, *what can I buy her?* She sat back and thought about what to give Dorothy, and then her mind went back to the time she was eighteen and what it was that she had been given.

Then it dawned on her and she knew what to give her granddaughter. She told Simon that she was going to give Dorothy the brush, just as her grandmother had done for her so many years earlier.

"Tell me, Simon," asked Jane, "will I ever be able to hear you again after I have given her the brush?"

Simon told her that he would slowly leave her after she had told Dorothy all that had happened to her since she herself had been given the brush, but that one day she would see him as he was.

Jane could not get anything more out of him, and as she knew only to well after all these years that it was useless to ask anything more, she put the brush down.

There was a knock on her door and in walked Mary. "Dorothy told me that you were not looking too good and that she was very worried about you, Mother. Are you sure that you will be all right for tonight? Everybody is looking forward to seeing you."

"Of course I will be all right. You just run along now and I will be down shortly."

Mary left. It had felt so strange talking to her and seeing how much she had grown up. It was as if Mary was a stranger to her, yet she was her own flesh and blood. She now cursed the state of mind that had allowed all those years to slip away. Anyway, she was now fully aware of herself and was going to enjoy the birthday celebrations.

That evening she went down to the party and had a wonderful time, the best she had had in many a year, she chuckled to herself. Before she went back upstairs, she spoke to Dorothy. "Would you like to take me to my room? I have got your birthday gift and I wanted to give it to you by myself."

"Of course, Gran," said Dorothy, "I will help you." She had been wondering what her Gran had got her. Even her mum did not know, and she normally knew most things that went on.

Jane sat down on the edge of her bed and said, "Dorothy, come and sit next to me, I want to tell you something."

Dorothy sat down and held her grandmother's hand. "Are you sure you are all right, Gran?" asked Dorothy.

"Yes, I am all right, but would you bring that box from the table over there?

Dorothy handed the box to her grandmother and sat down again.

"Dorothy, this is your gift and when you have opened it I will tell you about it."

Dorothy opened the box and gave a gasp. "Oh

Gran, it is your special brush, it is so old and beautiful, this has meant so much to you."

As she held the brush she felt a warm glow coming over her, a relaxing feeling.

"Dorothy, I will tell you all I know about the brush, as it is yours now and I hope it will bring you all the comfort it has given to me."

Jane then told her granddaughter all about how she had gotten the brush on her eighteenth birthday from her grandmother, how it had passed from grandmother to granddaughter, and of course she told her about Simon. "Do not be afraid of him, he will now be with you for your lifetime."

"But what about you, Gran, will Simon never speak to you again?"

"Don't worry about me, I will be all right. Just guard your gift and whenever you need advice brush your hair and he will be there. Now off with you, it has been a tiring day and I feel very sleepy.

"Oh thank you, Gran, for the best gift I have ever had, sleep tight—night."

After Dorothy left Jane lay back on the bed and closed her eyes for a short time before getting undressed. Suddenly she felt a movement in her room, as if somebody was there. She sat up to see a young man looking at her.

"Who are you, what do you want?"

The man just smiled at her and said, "Don't you recognise me, Jane? I'm Simon!"

She was now so relaxed with him that she felt no fear at all. "Is it really you, Simon, can I really see you at last?"

"Yes, and I have a present for you—come with me, Jane."

She reached out and took his hand whilst he led her to the window. As she looked out, she could see all her old friends and in the middle of the crowd was her husband and her own grandmother!

"How is this possible, Simon? They are all dead now."

"Look at your bed, Jane, and you will see how." Jane turned around and on the bed was an old lady with a smile upon her face.

"That is me," she whispered, "that is me!"

"Yes, that's right, but look at yourself now!"

She turned to the mirror and there was a young beautiful girl of eighteen. "Simon, am I dead?" she asked.

"Yes, you died peacefully in your sleep and now you are home with all your loved ones."

Jane took his hand and went down to the garden.

The Bubble Man

Mrs Watson was busy in the kitchen. Her son James was outside in the garden, taking in the sunshine. The last year had been very hard for her, being on her own with James, who the doctors had given only two years to live.

After the accident that left him but a shell in a wheelchair, she had devoted her life to him. Next week he would be fourteen years old and she was determined to give him a very special gift, because although he could show very little response, she felt that he knew she loved him dearly.

She went out into the garden to see if he was all right and saw him looking at the flowers. *If only he could run and walk again!* she thought.

"Jimmy love, would you like a drink? I have some nice cool lemonade," she asked.

He looked round at her and smiled. He could still speak, although some words were difficult, but he

follow the path your breath takes you

could not move any other part of his body except for his right arm.

James waved his hand and said, "Thanks Mum, that would be great."

Mrs Watson went to fetch the beaker and, while she was pouring out the drink, she thought about what the doctors had said about her son.

"You do know, Mrs Watson, that Jimmy is only paralysed in his mind and that is what stopping him from getting better. Most of his brain stopped working after the accident and because it no longer controls much movement, his body is not functioning and he is wasting away.

"As far as we can tell, his brain is not damaged and it seems to be Jimmy's decision whether he lives or dies." From that day on she had tried very hard to discover why Jimmy seemed to have lost the will to live, but nothing she did seemed to get through the barrier he had built in his mind.

Eventually she had concluded that only her faith could cure him and that, in time, God would heal her son.

"Here you are, Jimmy, a nice drop of lemonade. Maybe you would like me to take you out around the park, you always liked that," she said.

He looked up at her and nodded. It was true, he had liked the park, but now it made him sad to be reminded of what he could no longer do.

He knew why his mother was taking him, but for all the love and concern she felt he knew it would not help him. He felt his boyish anger start to build up inside, and the words started to race around his mind. "It's not fair; I want to play, I want to be like other boys, why did that car hit me?"

He still felt angry as his mother got him ready for the park, wrapping a blanket round his legs as he sat in his wheelchair: he knew it wasn't her fault that he was like this but it was difficult to be patient with her fussing around him.

The park was just around the corner from their house and he knew all the paths she would take him down. First they would go past the swings, then past the slide, and finally they would sit on the bench near the pond and feed the wildfowl that had adopted the pond as their home.

As his mother started to feed the ducks, an old man walked past. Jimmy's first thought was to be suspicious of any stranger—he might be a thief and if he were to try to steal his mother's handbag, Jimmy could do nothing to help!

He watched the stranger as he walked past and was surprised to see a friendly smile on his face that said "Hi." The stranger walked past but then stopped, turned, and walked back to them. He looked directly at Jimmy and spoke to him. That surprised Jimmy, because everybody spoke to his mother rather than to him.

"Excuse me, young man, would you mind if I sat down on this seat? My old legs are not what they use to be."

Mrs Watson decided that the old man seemed harmless and invited him to sit with them.

"I'm sorry about my boy, but since he was injured in a car accident, he has been almost entirely paralysed." James found it difficult to take his eyes off the old man. In some ways he seemed ordinary enough, like anyone's grandfather, but there was something about him that Jimmy found strangely familiar.

As his mother carried on talking to the old man, Jimmy ceased to pay much attention. This had become his custom, but on this occasion he felt like yelling out: "Look, I'm here, please don't treat me as if I were part of this chair: talk to me!"

As if in reply, he heard a voice saying, "So you don't want to talk to me then?" He saw that the old man was looking directly at him. "My name is James, too, but most people call me Big Jim."

"Sorry," Jimmy said, "I'm not used to people talking to me, they normally talk to Mum about me as if I weren't here."

"That's all right, Jimmy," said the old man, "I know how you feel. Many years ago, I was in a condition like yours. Maybe one day I'll tell you about my experiences."

As the old man was talking, Jimmy felt a strong attraction growing inside him: he could see that his mum had also taken to him.

"Why have we never seen you before?" Jimmy asked. "We often visit this park. Are you new to this area?"

"Well, I have seen you many times, but you and your mum seemed to prefer to keep yourselves to yourselves, and I did not feel that I should intrude."

The old man was right, they had been in a little world of their own: but what a small world it was!

James suddenly started to feel tired and said to his mother, "I would like to go home now, Mum, I think I've had enough for today."

"All right Jimmy, we will get on off home now and you can have a little nap before tea," his mother replied.

As they turned to depart, James asked the old man whether he would be there in the park the following day.

"Yes, I will certainly be here if you would like to see me again. Perhaps you should ask your mother first, however—she may have other plans."

"Mum, can we come again tomorrow?"

"I will see, but regardless, it will not be before lunch. How would it be if I brought us a picnic? Big Jim might like to join us!" she said, turning to the old man with a smile.

"I will see you tomorrow then—bye Little Jim," Jimmy said as he laughed.

That night Jimmy found it hard to sleep; there was something about the old man, something warming and familiar but strange as well. He found it hard to wait for tomorrow to come.

He then realised that for the first time since the accident he was looking forward to something. Perhaps it was because the old man had treated him as a person and not as an object of pity.

As he lay in the darkness, he felt a stirring within his mind. *Could it be true that something unusual is happening to me? Am I getting to know somebody new only to lose them again?* He felt a shiver of fear and sadness in his mind that was replaced by anger and resentment, a new sort of energy that started to fight against the invisible cords that tied him to his chair.

"No more—enough, enough!" he shouted. "I want to be me again."

At that moment a picture came into his mind, a picture of the old man called Big Jim saying, "You won't be afraid anymore."

With that message in his mind, Jimmy drifted quietly to sleep until the next morning, when he awoke to hear his mother drawing the curtains and saying, "Wake up, Jimmy! You sleepy-head, it is nearly eleven o'clock and I've got to get you and our picnic ready for the park today."

As his mother pushed his chair through the park towards their favourite bench, he could see Big Jim sitting there, waiting for them. "So you got here then, you two," he said, offering a helping hand with James's chair.

As he did so, James could not help but notice that the old man had brought a worn leather bag. Seeing the boy's attention drawn to it, Big Jim said, "Do you want to know what is in it?"

James did not know why, but for the first time in a long while he felt a strong curiosity: he did need to know what was in the bag. "Yes please, go on, show me what's in it."

Big Jim undid a large brass buckle and brought out a jar containing a pale green liquid. Next, out came a stick about as long as a pencil with a ring on the end.

"Have seen anything like this before, Jimmy?"

the old man asked. "I used to have one years ago, it's a kiddies' bubble toy. You know, you dip the ring into some soapy water and it makes bubbles when you blow gently through it."

Young Jimmy felt a sense of disappointment at the sight of this childish toy. He had hoped that Big Jim would have thought of something more interesting than that. "You would be right, Jimmy," said the old man, "but this bubble ring is different: it has magical powers. Anybody who believes in himself or herself can use it to go into the world of the bubbles."

Jimmy felt a strange resentment rising up inside him, he felt as if he was being treated as a young child, and he was to be fourteen next week!

Big Jim could see James's thoughts reflected in his face and he seemed to sense the boy's disappointment.

He got up and walked around to face young Jimmy. Bending down to him he said, "Listen to me, lad, you should believe in magic, the magic that everybody has inside them. Even your mum has it—don't you, Mrs Watson?"

"I suppose I did when I was a child, but that was years ago and things were different then, like at Christmas time—now that was magical," she replied.

James looked at his mother and could see in her eyes that she was telling the truth. He turned back to Big Jim and said, "No, I don't believe in magic; how many times do you think I've wished to get out of this chair, to be able to play as other children do.

You don't understand what it is like to be trapped like this day after day!"

"Listen to me, young Jim," Big Jim said, looking Jim straight in the eye. "Will you trust me? Within ourselves we have our own world and it develops as we get older, helping us to cope with the outside world in which we live.

"Your inside world has a wall round it that has been built to protect your mind from the effects of your accident. Behind that wall is the real Jimmy, the Jimmy I am talking to at this moment, not the empty shell that sits in this wheelchair. Let me help you to see the wall and then to punch a hole in it.

"If you will smash the wall that imprisons your mind, your body can come back to life. Of course if you want to stay as you are that is your choice, but the boy I am talking to wants to escape from his prison. I will tell you what I went through when I was your age, but that's for another day."

Young Jimmy looked at this strange but familiar old man. He was right, yes, for some strange reason he did trust him, even though he had only met him the day before. *Yes, I will go along with his magical bubbles and see what happens*, Jams decided.

"Big Jim," said James, "I cannot promise to understand what you are going to do, but I want to make my fourteenth birthday the day I take the first brick off my wall."

"Okay, let's start," said Big Jim. "Take this stick; dip the ring into the jar; and blow a bubble, a big one. As you blow it, try following the path your breath takes until you are inside the bubble in your mind's eye. Now look around you and see all the lights changing: now you are in your own world, young Jim."

Jimmy could see many shapes; they were changing with his thoughts. It felt so strange—he was alone but he could hear Big Jim talking to him, his reassuring voice calming his thoughts.

It seemed like an hour or more had passed when he heard Big Jim's voice calling him. "Come on, Jimmy, close your eyes and think your way back to where I'm sitting here, next to your mother."

Jim opened his eyes and the daylight dazzled him, causing him blink.

"Well," said Big Jim, "what did you think of the world inside the bubble?"

Jimmy could not answer straight away. His mind was fixed on what he had experienced—it was a new and wonderful world. He knew now that here was a way he could find himself, the real self
that had been locked away for so long.

Yes, the old man was right, the first brick had come down.

Over the next few months, Big Jim took Jimmy on many a trip to see the wonders in the land of the bubble. He showed him how, by thought, he could paint his own world through the rainbow hues of the bubble and so develop himself.

He also showed him how to make the special mixture to form the bubble.

His mother saw the change in him and was

delighted. He became brighter and was beginning to take more of an interest in other people as the months went by.

※※※※

The months turned into years and as his twentieth birthday approached, he started to remember how he had felt that day, five years previously, when he first met Big Jim.

He was now free from his wheelchair and able to walk again; no more frustrating inability to express feelings. He felt the growing strength of a young man, a young man taking charge of his life again. It was shortly before his twentieth birthday when, one day, he heard his mother call out to him, as was her custom. "Come on, Jimmy—if we are going to meet Big Jim in the park today we have got to hurry."

"Okay," Jimmy yelled back, "I'm just putting my shoes on, I'll be down in a minute. As he came downstairs he noticed his old wheelchair tucked under the stairs and suggested to his mother that as it was no longer needed, that they might take it down to the local hospital to help some other unfortunate.

This they did on their way to the park, although the chair was not needed at the hospital. It was passed on to an 'old folks' home' where it was immediately put to further service.

James and his mother made their way to the park and to their usual meeting place with Big Jim.

He was not there when they arrived and after some time, it became apparent that he wasn't coming. They then came to realise how little they knew about him—they didn't even know where he lived!

They had been so wrapped up in their own troubles that they had never paused to consider that their friend might have any problems of his own.

The afternoon turned to evening, the sun casting long shadows over the park.

"He's not going to come today, Mum, we'd better go home. Do you think something could have happened to Big Jim?"

"Perhaps, but for now we'll go home for tea and see what tomorrow brings."

The next day, the day after, and the rest of that week, James and his mother waited in vain for Big Jim to visit the park.

As he had arrived in their lives, without warning, so it seemed, had he departed. James and his mother felt helpless to do anything about it: nobody they knew had apparently ever met their friend and none of the usual enquiries led to any trace of Big Jim.

As the years went by, James never forgot what Big Jim had told him. "Life is inside you, as well as on the outside; to escape to the inside world, all you have to do is to make that bridge. The rainbow colours of the bubbles show you the path and inside it are the materials for your path and your rainbow bridge. Never forget this, Jimmy."

Many years later, as he was himself experiencing the frustrations of old age, all that had happened to him as a child now seemed so long ago. James had become something of a recluse since his mother's death years earlier, and he now lived alone, earning a reasonable living writing books.

※※※※

Unaccountably, he awoke one morning with irresistible urge to take a walk in the park. He had lost the habit many years previously, but that morning, he had to go. It was strange.

He got dressed, had a quick cup of tea, and walked to the park. It had not changed much since he was a boy. The trees were taller, although the park as a whole seemed smaller, and as he followed the familiar path, he noticed how it had worn in places, with patches of new tarmac filling the holes.

As he approached the old bench, he could see that a woman was seated there and that she was talking to a small boy who was wrapped in a blanket and sitting in a wheelchair. The two people seemed strangely familiar and the short hair on the back of Jimmy's neck prickled as he considered whether he should introduce himself.

He walked past the bench and smiled to see their reaction. It felt good. He then turned round and walked back to the bench.

James looked at the boy and then said, "Excuse

me, young man, would you mind if I sat down on this seat? My old legs are not what they used to be. My name is James, too, but most people call me Big Jim."

Printed in the United Kingdom
by Lightning Source UK Ltd.
108892UKS00001B/276